The 4th Floor Lounge

Amanda Hamm

ISBN: 978-0-98506593-5

For my husband,
who doesn't believe anyone hasn't seen *Star Wars*.

Chapter 1

I was pretending to be asleep when she moved in. Katherine. My new roommate. I don't think she ever knew that I wasn't really asleep. She never knew that I owed her a thank you for sending me to the 4th floor lounge. I didn't know when we parted that we would never see each other again.

If Katherine had any doubts about my pretending they were probably put to rest a few weeks later when I scared her by really sleeping through a fire drill. She had thought for a few seconds that I might be dead. Doesn't every college student harbor a secret fear that his or her roommate will die in the middle of the night?

No? Oh. Me neither.

Katherine was my second roommate. Things with my freshman year roommate hadn't exactly… worked out. She was a talker. I was not. She didn't understand that I found it exhausting to talk to her for hours at a time about… nothing. She felt I was being rude, or cruel even, when I picked up a book with her in the room. Especially if it wasn't directly related to a pressing school assignment. I suppose the best thing you could say about my year with Beth was that it made me a better student. Most of my work became due "tomorrow." The worst thing you could say was that it made me a better liar.

By the end of the first semester, Beth had found a small group of friends who were better suited to her personality. I had not. Three or four girls would gather in our room and pretend I wasn't there. I was completely fine with that. They, however, seemed freaked out that I could read, write or watch TV as though they weren't there. They spent a lot of time trying to make each other laugh. One would say something and the others would laugh while casting shifty glances my way to see if I was also laughing. They seemed annoyed with my eavesdropping if I cracked a smile and offended if I didn't. But even though they were in my space, I was not in their world. I couldn't laugh at reminiscences of things I hadn't seen and most of their jokes seemed to be at the expense of one guy or another. I understood guys like I understood talkers.

Near the end of the school year, when the housing forms came for the following year, there was a box you could check to keep the same roommate. I didn't check the box. I didn't have to ask Beth to know that she didn't check the box either.

I was determined to make a better start with my second roommate. I received the assignment a few weeks before the start of my sophomore year. I knew her name was Katherine and I knew her phone number. Cold-calling someone I had never met was pretty high on the list of things I didn't want to do. It was probably even higher than stepping on something sharp while barefoot, but not quite as high as letting a spider crawl on my arm.

Fortunately, I also had her email address. I decided to wait until just one week before move-in day to see if she would contact me first. I had left my phone number off the form to avoid being blindsided by small talk. But she could email me if she wanted to. I don't know if she wanted to, but she did not. Eventually I felt I couldn't put it off any longer. I sat down at the computer to think of an email that would make me seem friendly and welcoming and not weird without actually revealing any personal information. Other than the fact that I was bringing a TV and not a refrigerator.

The message was four sentences long and took me almost an hour to compose. Her reply was even shorter, saying something about looking forward to meeting me. You never know about tone in writing so I wondered if she was being sarcastic.

I left my parents' house mid-morning on a Monday. We moved in on Monday. Classes started Wednesday. In between, I was supposed to make friends with my roommate and catch up with all the friends I had missed over the summer. Two days would not be nearly enough time for one of those tasks and way too much time for the other. The drive was almost an hour. Short enough that I could come home on weekends if I wanted (something I had done most weekends that Beth had not) and still far enough away from home that I "had" to move into the dorms.

I stopped for a burger and ate it in my car before pulling into the unloading zone. I had less stuff than the previous year, but it still took more trips because my parents weren't there to help. I left the door open while I was going back and forth, and then closed it while I was unpacking. No one needed to see my mess. I didn't just close it so Katherine would need to use her key and give me a few seconds warning.

I was done arranging my side of the room by dinnertime. Or what should have been dinnertime, but I wasn't hungry. I did need something to drink and thought about going to the bookstore. I would need books and they also sold pop. I didn't know if I might also need an excuse to leave the room after Katherine arrived.

I found a vending machine and spent the next half hour pacing my newly configured room while drinking a Coke and trying not to think of all the ways my configuration might annoy Katherine when she arrived. My empty bottle rattled around the otherwise empty recycling bin by the door as I picked up the remote for the TV. Then I went back to pacing the room and thinking about how I'd have to turn off the TV and stop pacing when Katherine arrived.

I didn't normally go to bed so early. I was worn out from all the unpacking and pacing. I had just gotten into bed and was watching TV when Katherine came in. It was nearly 10 pm. I wanted to ask her why she was arriving so late when I knew from her address that the drive couldn't have been more than three hours. But I didn't ask. I didn't say anything. I pretended I was sleeping. It was easier than letting her think she had woken me up. It was easier than talking to someone for the first time while I was wearing pajamas. Sure, it was only an oversized T-shirt. But it was a nightgown I had been wearing in my own bed in my own home for years before I knew her and it felt like letting her in. So I didn't.

When she left the room the first time to fetch another load of boxes, I turned on the sleep timer so she would think I had done that before I went to sleep. I went to sleep for real before she was done unpacking.

The room looked really strange when I woke up. It was full of things I didn't recognize, including the stranger snoring in the next bed. It was a good thing I really could sleep through anything. I looked at Katherine for a moment. I could see only the back of her head, which included straight blond hair. Her hair was darker near the roots and very pale on the ends that spilled over the side of the bed.

I needed to get up. I was feeling the effects of having skipped dinner. My toes missed the plush carpet in my own bedroom as I crept over to the closet on the flat utilitarian threads in my dorm. I traded my nightgown for a pink-striped sundress and slipped my feet into a pair of sandals. I wore dresses often when the weather was nice. I thought they were pretty and that it might help. But mostly I wore dresses because it was easier than matching tops and bottoms. I didn't want to have to think about my clothes.

The halls were quiet as I made my way down to the dining hall for breakfast. Not that I was surprised that most people were sleeping in on a day with no classes. Only some areas of the dining hall were open, but I had no trouble finding a few things I liked. I thought about putting something on my tray to take back to Katherine. I had no idea what time she might wake up. I considered a bagel. That wouldn't have to be eaten right away. But what if Katherine didn't like bagels? What if she only liked them with certain toppings and I got the wrong one? What if she was allergic to wheat? What if she usually skipped breakfast? What if almost all those things were true and she felt she had to eat it anyway to spare my feelings?

It wasn't difficult to talk myself out of trying a nice gesture. I didn't know how not to.

I intended to eat my own bagel at one of the smaller tables by the windows. Alone. That wasn't weird. Most of the dozen or so students there were eating at tables by themselves. Unfortunately, I had to change my plan. One of those individuals, a guy wearing a sweaty tank top and running shoes, called me honey and invited me to join him. When I walked past him as though I had been already on my way back to my room, he yelled after me something about breaking his heart. I knew better.

But now I was going to have to eat in the dark so I wouldn't disturb Katherine. She began to stir shortly after I had finished my breakfast and was trying to decide what to do next. I heard her say that I could turn on the desk light if I wanted.

Oh, yeah. I had forgotten about the small lights near the desks. The overhead light was generally so much more convenient. Unless, of course, your roommate happened to be sleeping. I flipped the switch and mumbled my thanks. Trouble was, I still couldn't think of anything to do now that I could see the empty desk. Maybe I should have picked up some books after all. Katherine stretched and sat up. From the front, she was a fairly average looking girl whose skin hadn't quite cleared up. We introduced ourselves from across the room. It worked because it was a very small room. She apologized for getting in so late. An accident had blocked her path for more than two hours. After a few minutes of chit chat, she excused herself to shower and forage. Not necessarily in that order. Apparently, she did eat breakfast, but not in the room so I didn't know if she liked bagels.

I went for a walk until it was time for the bookstore to open. Two guys whistled at me before I got there. One from a car and one from the sidewalk across the street. I ignored both of them.

I dropped my newly purchased books in my room – Katherine wasn't there – and then went to the library. I was an English major. There were two novels on my booklist and I hoped to check them out before anyone else did to avoid buying them. I was in luck.

I started reading one of them as soon as I got back to the room. Katherine was out most of the day. We talked a bit more in the evening, with the TV on, and I thought it went well. She seemed nice. She seemed normal. More normal than I was anyway. We shared the room for almost a week before she explained the studying rule.

Chapter 2

Katherine may as well have called it the go away rule, except that that might have been rude. It turned out that the studying rule had been what came between Katherine and her freshman roommate. The other girl hadn't understood the importance of this rule, hadn't had enough respect for it, hadn't appreciated that it was as important to Katherine as actual studying.

Early in her first year, Katherine had met someone. His name was Caleb. By Christmas, they had "gotten serious." She was referring of course to a physical relationship. She shared more than a few details about that with me. And I had felt that introducing myself in my pajamas might have been too intimate.

Katherine hung a whiteboard on our door. Anytime she wrote "studying" on the board, that meant Caleb was visiting. It meant that I should not come in unless it was really, really important and then only if I knocked first. She wanted to know if I could handle that. I wanted to know if I had a choice. I didn't ask. I told her I'd try.

I met Caleb the day after she explained everything to me, wishing the whole time that I didn't know what I knew about him.

He also had blondish hair. I thought he and Katherine almost looked like they could be brother and sister. I didn't tell them that. I was on my way to class and didn't have to talk to him very long. When I got back, the sign said studying.

I sighed and lugged the black messenger bag on my shoulder down to the dining hall for an early dinner. Our room was on the 3rd floor and the dining hall was on the 1st. I wished I had known I wouldn't be able to unload my books before I had climbed two flights of stairs. I could have taken the elevator, but normally I like stairs. Normally, I'm not going up them just to go back down.

At least I got to eat by the window. Yes, alone. The window tables were small and round and seemed to me to be intended for solo dining. I don't know why they each had a second chair.

Katherine and I continued to get along fine those first few weeks. I suppose it helped that we didn't spend a lot of time together. I only bumped into the studying sign two more times. I assumed Katherine was spending a lot of time in Caleb's room.

It was almost a month into the school year when I bumped into the sign a fourth time. I don't know why I remember that it was the fourth time. Maybe I'm wrong about that. I just know it was the first time I didn't know what to do with myself. I had written a very nice paper that afternoon. Really. I'm not the only one who thought so. I got an A. I worked hard on that paper and then went to have dinner by the window. I ate spaghetti and didn't get any on my dress. I was going back to my room to relax when I found that it was closed due to studying.

I could have gone down to the computer lab. But I had just spent two hours in there working on that paper. I could have gone back for dessert. I wasn't hungry. Not even for ice cream. I tried to think if there was anyplace else I could go without leaving the building. There were bathrooms at either end of the hallway. No. There was a laundry room. I think I might have had enough clothes waiting to fill a load, but those clothes were in my room where I couldn't go because of all the studying. Then I remembered the lounge. The computer lab was at the end of the hall on the 1st floor. On the 2nd, 3rd and 4th floors… there were lounges. I had never been to the lounge. It seemed like a place to go to lounge, you know, with people. I didn't have any people to bring to the lounge. But I also didn't have anywhere else to go. I figured it wouldn't hurt to check it out.

As I started down the hall, I felt the phone in my purse buzz. I thought it was probably Erin. She had good timing.

What do you mean "Who's Erin?" I only said I didn't have any people to bring to the lounge. I never said I didn't have *any* people. Erin and I were best friends in high school. She was the only one I was still in contact with. Most of my high school friends were sort of friends of convenience. They were people who seemed like my friends because we talked and even laughed together because we happened to sit next to each other in a certain class. But Erin and I found things to do together after school and on weekends, too.

Erin went to a different college though. She kind of had to. She got a music scholarship. Erin played the cello. She played it well. Hence the scholarship. You don't say no to a full ride just because it leaves your friend looking like she doesn't have any friends. If only those people who thought I didn't have friends, if anyone thought about me at all, could see me pulling out my phone to read Erin's text.

It said: `I have decided to nickname my Calc prof Mr. Flat Earth.  I'm not telling you why.`

That was typical. Erin tried pretty hard to amuse me with her texts. A lot of them involved things she wasn't going to tell me. She always spelled out all the words. I loved Erin's use of punctuation. That was one way we could be weird together. But then, we were kind of new to the whole having a cell phone thing.

Erin was not allowed to have one in high school. It had something to do with her church. She didn't understand it herself and so couldn't explain it to me. I went to a Catholic church. Cell phones were not against the rules there as long as you turned them off during the mass. I didn't have a problem remembering since I didn't have a phone either. My parents didn't forbid it. I would have had to pay for it myself though and decided it wasn't worth it.

As far as I could tell there were only three reasons one needed a phone. The first was to send text messages. The second was to receive text messages. And the third was to talk to other people about all the texts you were sending and receiving. I figured that the only people I'd send and receive texts with were Erin and possibly, occasionally, my parents. The only people I'd want to talk to about those messages would have been Erin and possibly, never, my parents. As long as Erin didn't have a phone, I didn't either.

Just before we started at different colleges, Erin talked me into picking out phones together. I had to promise not to let her parents know and it was just about the most rebellious thing we ever did together. I stopped just outside the lounge to type out a reply. It said: `Why not Mr. Flat Head?`

I dropped the phone back into my purse and poked my head into the lounge. The door was in the middle of the room. To my right, where I looked first, were three round tables. Each had four chairs and only one person. Each of those three people was hunched over books and their backs were to me. They seemed to be resolutely not noticing me poking my head inside the door. But then I glanced to my left and realized that I needed to stop taking everything personally. They were actually resolutely not noticing the incredibly amorous couple on a couch over there.

I pulled my head back into the hallway. That lounge was not going to work. I didn't think I could be as good at not noticing things as those three other people. Especially when I was trying so hard not to think about why I couldn't go back to my room. But that was the 3rd floor. There were two more lounges directly above and below me. Perhaps I shouldn't give up yet. I walked into the stairwell and considered briefly whether I should go up or down. I chose to go up to the 4th floor lounge. In hindsight, I'm very, very glad I chose to go up.

****

I looked into the 4th floor lounge and tried to get a sense of the whole room at once. That way I wouldn't be surprised by anything happening on only one side. It looked safe so I went in.

The furniture was the same as on the 3rd floor. The same three tables on the right and the same big couch on the left. The couch was near the middle of the room facing a TV in the corner. I couldn't see what was playing. I recognized the sounds of Family Feud.

In the far left corner was an armchair with very wide arms. It was orange. The couch was orange. Some people might have said brown, but those people would have been wrong. If I wanted to be specific, I'd call it burnt orange. I'm sure I had a crayon when I was little called burnt orange that would have exactly matched that couch. The chair, too, as a matter of fact. It was the same color as the couch, but I was kind of focused on the couch because there was a guy sitting at one end of it. He was the only other person in the room and if I had to pick a crayon color for him it would have been sunshine yellow.

I walked around the back of the couch to sit at the far end of it. We each smiled slightly to acknowledge the other. Then he wordlessly offered me the remote by holding it in my direction. I liked how his eyes asked the question and I shook my head in a way that I hope said, "I don't mind watching Family Feud" and not "You were here first so I'll put up with your lame show."

We sat in silence through a commercial break. There was something about that guy that was drawing more of my attention than the TV. He was wearing jeans and a plain black T-shirt. His sandy brown hair was a bit curly. It was long enough that it stuck up here and there. It wasn't anything like what anyone would call a 'fro. It just looked like hair that had a mind of its own and I respected that. It looked good on him. But I was trying to look like I hadn't noticed. I didn't know why he was harder to ignore than most people.

Mostly I was glad that I had found a place to go. The atmosphere in the 4th floor lounge was so much more welcoming than the atmosphere in the hallway outside the room I wasn't allowed to enter. I had gotten almost completely comfortable and relaxed after what had been kind of a long day when the guy next to me spoke for the first time.

He said, "Will you marry me?"

Chapter 3

I jumped.

I knew he wasn't talking to me because I had been listening to the TV. The host had just asked the contestants to name a question that someone might be nervous before asking. "Will you marry me?" was an obvious answer. It was the number one answer. And the guy next to me had said it before anyone else. Which is why I was startled not by what he said, but simply because I hadn't expected him to say anything. At least, not out loud. So I jumped and then sat there embarrassed because I had jumped. He looked a little embarrassed as well, presumably because he had made me jump.

I'm not sure if he couldn't think of any more answers to the question or if he was giving me time to recover. Either way, it was quiet for a few minutes. When the host read the next question, I looked at my couchmate. He opened his mouth for a moment before talking. That might have been his way of preparing me.

Then he said, "Lilac."

I shook my head and laughed, pretty sure he had given a bad answer on purpose. Then he looked at me expectantly, as though daring me to give a better answer.

I said, "White." White was number two.

We sat through an episode and a half of Family Feud. Each occasionally saying an answer, occasionally nodding at the other's. It might have been the fastest 45 minutes of my life. He slid the remote towards me on the couch when the second episode ended and he got up to leave. He stopped at the doorway and turned to look at me. I thought maybe he was going to say something. He just sort of half-waved and disappeared.

I left the TV on when I left the room a few minutes later. I had begun to wonder if I could go back to my room yet. Caleb was gone when I got there. So was Katherine. I gathered my things to take a shower.

I started showering before bed in high school so I could sleep a bit later in the mornings. Classes were less early in college. I still showered at night because those who took showers in the mornings usually ended up waiting in line. And because my hair was long and thick and took forever to dry. I know. I timed it. I didn't want to spend forever with a hair dryer in the morning and if I didn't the wetness from my hair would spread to the entire back side of my clothes. And the front if those soggy ends made their way over my shoulders. No one wants to arrive at class looking like she walked in the rain when everyone knows it isn't raining. My hair, as well as the rest of me, looked better dry.

Dry, it was thick and slightly wavy and auburn. Auburn. Not red. No, I was not sensitive about the color of my hair. It was just that certain people, my mother, insisted on saying that I had red hair when I did not. There was nothing wrong with having red hair; saying I had red hair was wrong. It was mostly brown with some rosy tints. When I corrected people, it was about me getting facts straight and not about me being vain.

I walked back to my room with my towel wrapped around my hair. I couldn't keep it up there for long because it was very heavy. It helped soak up some of the water though. By morning, my hair would be nearly entirely dry.

Some of the other girls would walk back from a shower with their towels wrapped around their bodies. Some of the guys would prowl the girls' hallway in the morning hoping to catch glimpses of those girls. I suspected that was why most of them wore towels. That didn't make a lot of sense to me, but it wasn't that hard to bring clothes, or at least a robe, to the bathroom so I figured there must be a reason.

****

My classes were starting out not terribly. The biggest problem so far was that most of them seemed smaller than my freshman classes. It was harder to blend in with fewer people in the room. And I had one really scary professor who wanted everyone to call her by her first name. That was so not going to happen. Like I was going to go up to some woman with gray hair and a booming voice who seemed to know so much and say, "Hey, Susan. Nice day?"

It shouldn't really be a problem since I planned to continue to go out of my way not to talk directly to any of my professors. Unless they made me say something in class and then I certainly would not call them by name. But now I had to make sure I remembered what it was I wasn't calling her just in case.

I was coming back from the anomaly of being taught Shakespeare by "Susan" the next time I ran into that studying sign. I decided to go straight to the 4th floor lounge. I was suddenly glad I was wearing one of my favorite dresses. It was cornflower blue with tiny white flowers and elbow length sleeves. The material was thick so I could wear it a little further into the autumn than some of my other dresses. We were only a few days into October, but mornings were already getting cold.

I passed sweaty tank top guy from that first morning on my way to the stairwell. I guessed he lived on my floor because I passed him somewhat regularly. He almost always had clean clothes on, but I still referred to him in my head as sweaty tank top guy. He sighed dramatically when he saw me as though he still couldn't believe that I "broke his heart" that first day. That was his typical behavior.

My typical response was to ignore him completely. But on that particular afternoon, I was in a weirdly happy mood. Sort of hopeful for some reason. So I acknowledged sweaty tank top guy with a small nod and I said hi.

That was it. Just hi. I've been accused of being antisocial for not saying hi so I kind of thought it was expected. I didn't know it could be construed quite so encouragingly.

When I entered the 4th floor lounge, it was completely empty except for me and sweaty tank top guy who had apparently followed me there because I said hi. I put my book bag onto one of those three round tables as I prepared to sit down. I thought I might as well try to do some work. Sweaty tank top guy sat at the next table, facing me. He hadn't brought anything with him. He tipped his chair back on two legs and laced his fingers behind his head.

"So…" he said. "You're talking to me now?"

I had said hi. All I said was hi. I opened my bag and pulled out a binder while he waited for me to respond. I looked at him somewhere near his shoulder and shrugged. "I haven't been not talking to you. I just don't know you."

"Oh!" He let the front legs of his chair fall to the floor and leaned forward. "I'm Brady."

I nodded and began flipping pages in my binder.

Brady said, "This is the part where you tell me your name."

"It's Charlotte."

"Hey, like the spider?"

No, not like the spider. Why couldn't people assume I had been named for a city or a queen or at least a human character from a book, which was the truth? It seemed the only people who didn't associate my name with an arachnid were the ones who were a little confused and thought the pig was the title character. Because pigs have webs. Although another truth was that I'd rather have been named for a pig than a spider.

I found the page I was looking for. I had an essay to write and thought I might write down a few thoughts. But sweaty tank top guy, I mean Brady, didn't seem to be taking the hint.

"What's your major?" he asked.

"English."

"You a freshman?"

"Sophomore."

"Cool," he said. "I'm a sophomore, too, but still undecided." He paused for a moment. I turned back to my assignment thinking maybe we were done with the small talk. I was sort of right. The next thing he said was, "So you gonna go out with me now?"

"Why would I do that?" I asked. I was serious.

"Ouch!" Brady put his hand over his heart as though I had wounded him. Then he cocked his head and said, "Why wouldn't you?"

"Well… I still don't know you."

He actually laughed at that. "That's exactly why you *would* go out with me. So that you can get to know me."

I had to admit he had a point. But not out loud. I didn't say anything out loud. I was trying to decide if he was serious.

"Come on. You've got to say yes. I've only just recovered from the last time you rejected me."

Now I knew he wasn't serious. His eyes were wide and he plastered on a winning smile. Brady was a very good-looking guy who obviously knew he was a very good-looking guy. I could tell he was more interested in proving that I would go out with him than he was in actually having me go out with him. It was a good thing I was immune to his charms. That was my brother's fault. He had too many friends.

I just said, "I don't think so."

"Really!?" Brady hung his head. He stood up slowly as though I had knocked out his will to go on. He turned to me before he got to the door and put on that winning smile one more time. "I'll tell you what," he said, "I plan on having dinner tonight right around 5:30. You can just meet me in the dining hall if you change your mind. I'll be watching for you. I think I've been watching for you my whole life."

I tried to keep the eye roll to myself as I told him I didn't plan on changing my mind.

"At least think about it?" He put his hands together as though he were begging. At the same time, there was a trace of sincerity in his eyes that made me want to believe that was his first real offer. But I didn't. I simply didn't. I skipped dinner altogether that night just to be sure.

Chapter 4

I had said that I wasn't in the habit of going up stairs just to go back down them. Over the next few days I was starting to find that this was no longer true. There were a few times that I walked up to the 4th floor lounge to see what was happening in there before going back down to my room. I carried a book with me to read in case I decided to go in. It was a Friday morning when I decided to go in.

I wondered if that big chair in the corner was comfortable. I took my book over to it. Sat down. Crossed my legs. Opened to the bookmark. Neither of the other people in the room said anything when I came in. There were two guys at separate tables who appeared to be doing homework. One of them was the guy who had watched Family Feud with me. I couldn't decide if I had ever seen the other guy before. He had kind of a pointy nose.

The room was very quiet for almost an hour. There was an occasional rustle of pages or a pen scratching at a word. Sometimes pointy nose guy clicked his pen. Not in a clicky-clicky-clicky annoying sort of way. He just turned it off while thinking and on again to write. Very consistently. I could now count that among the ways that I was not weird. The other guy kept bouncing his heel up and down on his left leg. I guessed that he must be working on a difficult assignment. People seemed to twitch when they were nervous or stressed.

My phone buzzed. I pulled it out to check. This was a really good time to look like I had friends. Erin was great. Her text said: `I'm thinking about wearing the blue shoes today. Talk me out of it.`

Erin had bought herself a pair of blue stilettos for her seventeenth birthday. She loved those shoes. She wanted to wear them often and also wanted them to last a long time. Sometimes she wanted me to remind her to save them. I thought they looked dangerous so I tried: `Twisted ankle?`

I was putting the phone back into my purse when I heard cards shuffling. I looked up. Pointy nose guy had packed up his books and pulled out a deck of cards. He looked from me to the other guy. "Anyone up for a study break?"

I looked at Family Feud guy and then back to pointy nose guy. I didn't say anything right away. He was looking at me, but I still wasn't sure if he meant to include me in his question. I was kind of used to not being included. But then Family Feud guy said, "What can we play with three?"

Pointy nose guy thought for a moment. "Rummy?"

Family Feud guy nodded and then looked at me. They were both looking at me. I realized I wanted to play Rummy so I said okay as I walked over to pointy nose guy's table. Family Feud guy sat down on his other side. We spent a few minutes making sure we were all going to be playing the same version of the game before the cards were dealt. I won the first round.

Pointy nose guy pulled out his notebook. "I have paper if you guys want to keep score."

I nodded. It seemed fair to give them a chance to catch up.

"Yeah, what should we play to?"

"500?"

I looked at my watch. I had a class in about 45 minutes. Family Feud guy noticed me checking.

"We could always come back later if you have to go before we're done," he said.

"Okay," I answered. That sounded like a wonderful idea.

Family Feud guy began to deal out a second hand while pointy nose guy opened the notebook. He held his pen over the page, clicked it, and looked up.

"What's your name?" he asked.

"Jason."

Jason. That was probably better than Family Feud guy. They were both looking at me again.

"Charlotte."

Pointy nose guy wrote our names on his score sheet, then looked up and said, "I'm Adam, by the way."

I extended my lead with the second hand and then it was my turn to deal.

"Awesome!"

"Hey, where'd you learn to do that?"

"My mom," I said. I blushed a little. I hadn't meant to show off. Several years earlier my mom had taught me how to bridge the cards. First you shuffle the cards and then you bend them back up so that they sort of float together instead of having to shove them together. That was the way I always shuffled cards. It wasn't very difficult, but I knew it looked kind of cool if you didn't know how. That was why I had wanted my mom to teach me. I shuffled them again and Adam asked if my mom had taught me any other tricks.

I smiled to myself. "Not really."

"Not really?"

"What do you mean by that?" Jason asked.

"Well… It's not a trick, but there is one thing that I always think of when I think of my mom and cards."

"Show us," Adam insisted.

Jason nodded eagerly. It seemed like they really wanted to know and I couldn't believe I was going to do it. "Put your hand on the table," I said to Adam.

"Like this?"

I nodded. Then I bit my lip as I shuffled the cards on the back of his hand. Both guys laughed.

"I told you it wasn't a trick." I had to defend myself. "It's just that I remember my mom doing that a lot when I was little. I would ask her to. I thought it felt funny."

"It does sort of tickle."

Jason put his hand on the table. "My turn."

I shuffled on his hand, too, and felt even sillier than I had the first time. They both wanted me to do it again. I thought we should get back to the game. After all, I reminded them, I was winning. They asked me not to rub it in and we continued. I kept a close eye on the score and on my watch. I started to worry when I got up to 420 points.

"You know, I really think I need to get going," I said.

"Your class is at 10:30?"

"Yeah."

"Oh, you have time," Adam said.

"Come on," Jason added, "one good hand and you can finish us off."

"No, really, I need to print something on my way. I need to go." I was totally lying. Thank you, Beth. But I wanted an excuse to see the guys again. I stood up and picked up my book and my purse. "Can we finish tomorrow?"

"That's Saturday, right?"

I nodded. "I have to work in the afternoon, but how about in the morning?"

Jason nodded.

"As long as it's not too early."

"Ten?" I suggested as I moved to the door like someone in a hurry. I got more nods from both the guys and backed out of the room. I grabbed my things from my room and went to class. I was going to be early, but I didn't care. I sat in the mostly empty classroom and sent Erin a text that said: `I am dominating` over two guys at the same time. No details for you.

When I turned my phone back on after class, she had sent me eight messages asking for details with varying forms of please attached.

****

I stared at my closet Saturday morning. In the dark because Katherine was asleep. It was cold enough that I might look more out of place than usual wearing a dress. But I'd have to change before I went to work anyway and I wasn't going outside before then. I didn't know if that made it okay. Probably not if I wasn't going to explain it to anyone. I wanted these two guys, my potential friends, to think I wasn't weird. I wanted to look nice. I didn't want to be too warm and make my cheeks get all pink. I wished I had some idea how to make a good impression on people without looking like I was trying so hard. I just put on a dress that I liked. Then I had breakfast and came back to brush my teeth. It was only 9:40. They would only know I was early if they were early. I went upstairs.

I stopped outside the door to the lounge. It was closed. The door was never closed. Ever. Even last year when I didn't go into the lounges, I was pretty sure I had never seen the door closed. I looked around. Should I wait for the guys in the hall?

No, someone might ask me what I was waiting for. And I wanted to know if there was something going on in the lounge that would prevent us from playing a game. I held my breath as I grabbed the knob and slowly began to push the door in. No one pushed back or yelled at me. I peered around the door and saw Jason standing next to the couch with his shoes off. He was looking guilty about something and also sort of… warm? He was also laughing so I went in and closed the door behind me.

"Um… what are you doing?"

"Promise you won't laugh?"

"You are."

"Good point. Okay, promise you'll be laughing *with* me."

I said I'd try. Laughing with someone sounded good. Laughing with Jason sounded great.

"Well, I was sitting here and for some reason I remembered that my mom used to yell at me all the time for jumping on the couch and… well, I couldn't remember doing it. I'm sure I must have jumped on the couch or she wouldn't have yelled at me and I must have enjoyed it or I wouldn't have kept jumping on it after she yelled at me and I just had this impulse to see if it was still fun."

"So you were in here jumping on the couch?" It was kind of hard to talk because I was laughing and trying not to laugh at the same time. I hated it when I laughed in front of someone I didn't know. It was not quite as fun as I thought.

Jason didn't seem to notice I was tense. He just said, "You're laughing with me now, right? *With* me?"

For some reason his concern helped me relax. I assured him I was laughing with him. Then I caught my breath and asked if it was fun.

Jason looked a bit sheepish, but then the grin returned. "You know, it was kind of fun. Do you want to try?"

I shook my head.

"I think you do," he said. He wiggled his eyebrows at me.

I thought he might be right. I did want to jump on the couch, but not by myself. I didn't want to look stupid in front of Jason. Or at least not any more so than I had when I shuffled cards on his hand. And I didn't want to get caught jumping on the couch. But I loved the idea of watching him have fun and if that's what it took… I decided to go for it. I said, "Only if you'll do it with me."

He nodded and stepped up on the couch while I took my shoes off. He held out his hand to help me onto the couch. I felt a shiver and I didn't know if it was from the risk of getting caught or just because he touched my hand. I mostly kept my hands to myself so I wasn't used to the sensation of someone else's skin.

Jumping on the couch was actually kind of fun… until there was a knock at the door. We had just enough time to climb off the couch again before it opened. It was Adam. He gave us a strange look as he asked if he could come in.

I waved him inside. "Yeah, we were just jumping on the couch."

"Jumping on the couch?" Adam closed the door behind himself as well. I was plenty embarrassed, but I was quick with the truth because I had just remembered some of the other things people did on those couches and I was afraid Adam would think he had walked in on me and Jason making out.

Adam took a few steps closer to us. "Really!?" he asked.

I shrugged. Jason shrugged.

Then Adam shrugged and took off his shoes, too. "When in Rome, right?"

Then all three of us stood on the couch. It only took two jumps before we heard a loud cracking sound and we jumped back to the floor. Adam landed on his shoes and hopped on one foot wincing in pain while Jason and I walked around the couch, inspecting it. It didn't seem to be caved in anywhere and nothing was sticking out. Whatever had snapped must be on the inside and staying there, for now.

Adam, whose foot seemed to have recovered, suggested that we test it. "Charlotte, you're the lightest. Sit on it a minute and see if it holds you."

I didn't like that plan. Jason rescued me. "No, no," he said. "It was my idea. I'll test it." He sat down slowly. Bounced gently in a few places. It appeared to work, but it now made a strange creaking sound whenever he moved that it hadn't made before. He stood up and looked at the couch. Then he said, "I'm thinking this is exactly why my mom used to yell at me for jumping on the couch."

I put my hand over my mouth to keep the laugh in. It didn't work. And it didn't work for either of the guys either. It was great. It was a more natural laugh. We had just created a bond between the three of us. It was an unspoken "don't tell anyone we broke the couch" bond. I felt a little guilty for being so happy about breaking the couch.

We put our shoes on and finished the game from the previous day. It did only take me one more hand to beat them.

Afterwards, we played three-way War because that was something else we hadn't done since we were kids. It was more fun than I remembered. Jason kept trying to cheat. He was really obvious about it so he wasn't really trying to cheat. He was just being funny. And I laughed more.

I was eliminated from War first and the guys celebrated their vengeance. Then Adam started letting Jason cheat so the game would end. We exchanged cell phone numbers before leaving so the three of us could get together again. I now had 200% more people who might potentially send me texts. Not counting my parents, of course.

Chapter 5

It took almost a week for me to meet Adam and Jason in the 4th floor lounge again. I wanted to suggest we meet again the next day, but I had to wait until Wednesday when Adam texted us to see if we could meet him in the afternoon. That time didn't work for me so I suggested Thursday. I tried not to feel bad that my suggestion didn't work for either of the guys. But we had first met on a Friday morning and that slot was still free. As long as it wasn't too early.

We met at nine. I expected cards again. Adam brought ping pong paddles instead. Panic struck. I had a terrible feeling that my complete lack of hand-eye coordination was about to sink my new friendships. Jason brought his breakfast. He had hit snooze at least one too many times and was eating a bowl of cereal when he came in. His hair was wet.

The ping pong experiment turned out not nearly as bad as I feared for a lot of reasons. Mostly related to the fact that it was more experiment than ping pong. We moved some chairs and gathered around one of the tables. The plan was to tap the ball around in a circle between us. The table had seemed a lot bigger when we used it for cards. We had to tap the ball very lightly from person to person, which made it a little easier for me to hit. The guys thought that made it too boring. And then I started to be afraid of being hit with a paddle.

Plan B was to use all three tables. We moved all the chairs into a corner and pushed the tables into something like a triangle. We each had our own table and tried to bounce the ball to someone else's table. The problem was that the tables were still round. This made a big hole in the middle of our triangle. I wasn't the only one knocking the ball into the hole. I was definitely doing it the most often though. Not on purpose. Adam accused me of aiming for the hole on purpose. I really wasn't. But then I started to wonder if maybe that was a good idea. Maybe if I aimed for the hole, I'd actually be able to keep the ball on the table.

Adam and Jason tried this idea before I could. They began to aim for the hole and couldn't seem to get the ball to drop. They thought it was a lot harder than it looked. Jason joked that maybe I'd just been showing off my hidden talent the whole time.

I felt bad about leaving them to move the tables back on their own. I should have helped. I was late for class anyway. I hated being late for class because everyone watched me enter.

****

We got together a few more times, not always on a Friday, but always in the 4th floor lounge. There were rarely other people in there and it was starting to feel like our space. Jason brought a different kind of card game to our space. It was called *David & Goliath*. It was harder than Rummy. He won several games in a row before Adam suggested we burn the game. I think he was kidding. Next time he showed up with a black plastic case, which I assumed was a different game. One that he was good at. But he plopped it on the table and said, "Charlotte, I want to ask you a favor."

I was curious so I said, "Okay?" I'm pretty sure I said it as a question.

"Will you give me a haircut?"

"What!?"

"A haircut. Will you cut my hair?"

He opened the case and inside I saw a set of clippers. I didn't know that was what it was called, but I had seen similar tools in use when my hair was being cut. Not on me though. They always used scissors on my hair. Something with a motor seemed a bit risky. I thought something like that should probably not be in my hands. But Adam seemed to be looking around the room for an outlet. That's when I realized he was serious. That's when I started laughing. That's when Jason walked in.

"Hey, guys," he said. "What's going on?"

I told him. "Adam seems to have lost his mind. That's all."

Jason looked between us with a puzzled look on his face.

I explained the situation. "He wants me to give him a haircut, and I'm pretty sure I'm not qualified to give haircuts." I turned back to Adam and added, "I work at Taco Bell, remember?"

"No, it's easy." He picked up the clippers and stretched out the cord a bit. Then he snapped some sort of attachment on the end. "You just put this on here, then you turn it on and run it over my head until all the hair is the same length."

"If it's that easy, why can't you do it yourself?"

"Well, I thought I could. That's why I brought the clippers to school with me. But then when I was actually going to, I realized that I couldn't figure out a way to see the back of my head so I wouldn't know if I got it all. And this part…" He held the clippers up to mime going over the back of his crown, "Just feels kind of awkward."

"And there's no one else who might actually know what they're doing?"

"I don't…" He glanced at Jason. "It just seems like a girl thing. I mean, I'm not trying to be sexist or anything, but my mom always does it so that's what I'm used to. Come on, Charlotte, it's bugging me."

I considered for a moment. I looked at his hair and realized that he was right. I don't know if he was right about the hair bugging *him*. But now that I looked at, it was kind of bugging me. It just seemed like it would look better a bit shorter. Mostly though, I figured that it was his head. If he wanted to walk around looking like I gave him a haircut then that was his prerogative. I shrugged, giving in.

"Awesome," he said. Adam pulled a chair over to the wall next to the outlet.

Jason pulled up a second chair nearby. He sat down and rubbed his hands together saying, "This ought to be a good show."

Normally, watching someone get a haircut is not a good show. I think he was excited about seeing me screw it up. Adam sat down as I stood behind him and took the clippers. "Are you sure there isn't anything you've forgotten to tell me? I just drive this thing all over your head?"

"That's it."

"Wait a minute. Isn't this going to make a mess?"

"That's why I brought this." Adam pulled a lint roller out of his pocket. I wondered how I hadn't noticed that he had a lint roller sticking out of his pocket. I guess I had been too busy staring at the clippers. "I'll pick up a lot of it with this and they vacuum in here every night anyway."

"Okay." I held the clippers near his head and prepared to flip the switch. "Last chance to back out," I said.

Jason smirked at me.

Adam said, "Quit stalling."

I took a deep breath and turned them on. They weren't very loud, just a gentle hum. The vibration was pretty strong though. It made my whole arm hum. I started at the back of his neck and pushed the clippers up through his hair. Watched the spray of cut hair drop over my hand and onto his shoulders and onto the floor. Moved the clippers over a bit and pushed them up again. More hair falling. Realized it would be easier if I put my left hand on his head to hold it steady. His hair was soft. It made my other arm tremble, too. I hadn't realized that giving a haircut would require me to stand so close. Felt stupid for not realizing that. Also felt warm all over for standing in Adam's space. I wasn't used to that. I knew my checks were turning a bit pink and hoped I was the only one to notice. Jason was watching me. I couldn't tell if he noticed. Felt like someone should say something. Felt like maybe I should say something, but I was still not a talker. The clippers tugged a bit. A topic.

"I'm not hurting you, am I?"

"What? No, of course not. Does it hurt when your hair gets cut?"

"I know, but… my hair cuts are a little less… robotic."

"Robotic?" Jason repeated.

Yeah, it was kind of a stupid thing for me to say. I couldn't think of a better word. Maybe motorized? It turned out to be a good thing to say anyway because it made us all smile. I could tell Adam smiled by the way his head felt in my hand. The smiles made the weird tension leave the room. I relaxed somewhat as I finished up. "Okay," I said, switching off the motor. My hand felt like it continued to vibrate for a few seconds. "I think I got it all. Jason, what do you think?"

"Hmm…" Jason stood up and came a few steps closer to inspect my work. "Yeah, I think you did a good job."

I congratulated myself on having not screwed up. At least not so badly that anyone noticed right away. That was good enough.

Then Adam stood up and offered his chair to Jason. "What do you think, man? You next?"

"Yeah, I'm a pro now." I taunted Jason with the clippers I was still holding.

“Sure,” Jason said as he pretended he was going to take the chair.

Adam was kidding. I was kidding. Jason was kidding. We all knew that we were all kidding. But three odd things happened anyway. The first was that I found myself wishing I could give Jason a haircut even though I knew it would ruin his wonderful hair. The second was that I realized I thought Jason had wonderful hair. The third was that for about half a second I was sure Jason looked tempted.

I handed the clippers to Adam who said he would handle the mess. There wasn’t quite as much hair on the carpet as I had anticipated. Jason and I took the two chairs back to the table while Adam brushed himself and some of the carpet with his lint roller. He collected and tore off several sheets worth so maybe his dark brown hair was blending in with the dark brown floor when I had surveyed the mess. Jason had brought a game and was setting it up. I was helping. Then I noticed that Adam had taken his shirt off to shake the hair out of it. He noticed me looking at him. He turned red. He quickly put the shirt back on. I can appreciate modesty. I also appreciated that he didn’t have anything to be embarrassed about. His shoulders were very strong.

Adam spent most of the game rubbing the back of his neck. I spent most of it thinking we should have used one of those barber cloths. I hadn’t thought of that sooner because I really didn’t know anything about giving haircuts. Now I knew a little bit.

Chapter 6

I stopped to read Erin's text on my way back from class. It said: `I am never eating there again. I'm not telling you where or why.`

I didn't know what that meant, which was of course her point. I decided to call her later to find out both where and why. I couldn't think of a quick reply when I was on my way to the 4th floor lounge. I always felt like I was in a hurry when I was going to meet Adam and Jason. Even when I was early.

We had been having a lot of fun together. We played a lot of games. If I was the kind of person who kept track, I'd say that I was leading in victories. But only if you didn't count ping pong or that bit of indoor Frisbee. They couldn't talk me into joining the indoor Frisbee. And I had been talked into giving someone a haircut. In the lounge. With an audience. I was pretty firmly opposed to games that involved throwing and/or catching.

Sometimes we rearranged the furniture in the lounge. Except for the couch. We were a little afraid of moving the couch. Once we turned all the tables upside down before we left. I'd like to say we did it because it was fun. Mostly we did it because it was something to do. That weekend there was a notice posted on the door from the cleaning staff asking whoever kept moving the furniture around to please stop moving the furniture around. We laughed when we saw it. But we also stopped moving the furniture.

Slowly I learned about the guys I tentatively called my friends. Adam was from Ohio like me. In fact, he had graduated from my high school's arch rival. I tried not to hold that against him. Jason was from Indiana. I tried not to hold that against him. He was a sophomore as well and Adam was a freshman. They were both majoring in Computer Science. Jason liked bagels.

I liked meeting Adam and Jason in the lounge because it was familiar and safe and quiet. I don't know why neither of them ever suggested we meet somewhere else. I think I would have met them somewhere else, as long as I didn't have to throw or catch anything while I was there.

I did bump into Jason outside once. He was walking to class with a guy who smiled too broadly and grabbed my hand when Jason introduced us. Smiley guy tried to pull me along in their direction and put on sad puppy dog eyes when I insisted that I couldn't. Jason asked him to "knock it off" and he did. I wished it had been that easy with Andy's friends.

My brother Andy was four years ahead of me in school, which meant he finished high school just before I started it. People always commented on how we looked so much like each other. I think we both looked more like our mom than our dad. No one ever commented about how we acted so much like each other. Because we didn't. I was the quiet, introverted one. An aunt once told me this was because I had an "old soul." I think that was a nice way of saying that I was weird. I don't know what she meant by it though. It's possible that it was not any nicer than saying I was weird.

On the other hand, Andy was a people person. He was a talker. When I was in 7th and 8th grade, he spent a lot of time talking to the steady stream of teenage boys who visited our house. A lot of those boys flirted with me mercilessly. Andy did ask them to stop, twice that I know of, but that only made them better at flirting with me behind his back. Despite some recent, um, developments I was too young for them. I was too young and they knew it. They only flirted to watch me turn bright red.

I hated it. I hated that they could embarrass me like that and I hated that they thought it was funny to embarrass me like that. I started high school knowing that some boys flirted just to be cruel and I didn't trust myself to be able to tell the difference. It was safer and easier to assume no one was serious. Even if that made them call me stuck up or ice queen or worse.

Then when I was in 11th grade, there was a boy in my math class that made me wonder. He sat a couple rows over. Not close enough that we talked or anything. Sometimes he seemed to be trying to catch my eye. I started to think that he might have been honestly trying to get my attention. And not so he could tell someone that he got my attention. But I didn't know, couldn't tell for sure, and then the school year was over. If he had been serious, he forgot about me over the summer.

Jason and Adam didn't seem to be in danger of forgetting about me. They were suggesting meet-ups at least as often as I was. And not because there were two of them. I mean each of them, individually, had planned at least as many meet-ups as I had. I was keeping track so I wouldn't look like the desperate one who always wanted to get together.

Once we taped an out-of-order sign on the TV even though it wasn't broken. We thought it might keep other people out. And we thought it was funny. I thought a lot of things were funny when I was with them. The fun lasted almost two months. It was December when things started to fall apart.

****

It was Adam. It wasn't Adam's fault, but it was Adam. He started to act… different. Sometimes we'd sit at a table to play a game and his knee would bump into mine. It didn't seem like an accident. Sometimes I could feel him looking at me. It was subtle, not like the overt flirtation I was used to, but I knew what he meant by it and I knew that he meant it. What I didn't know was how to handle it.

He texted me on a Tuesday just before 2pm. We all planned to meet at 2:30. He said he had some extra time and was heading to the lounge early. Said he would tell Jason. I believed that he told Jason. I also believed that he knew Jason would be coming directly from class at 2:30. I was in my room sort of working on homework and sort of counting down the minutes until 2:30. I stared at Adam's message for a long time. He wanted to talk to me alone and I knew that meant he had decided to make a move.

Part of me was curious. I liked Adam. He was nice and we had fun and I had seen him with his shirt off and hadn't minded at all. And let's face it, I was 19 years old and had only ever kissed one guy. I thought it was about time I kissed another one. But I couldn't kiss Adam just to see what it was like and then pretend it didn't change anything. I couldn't pretend that rejecting him wouldn't change anything either. I felt that my only hope was to avoid being alone with him long enough for things to sort of… blow over. Maybe he didn't like me the way he thought he liked me and if I was very careful he'd stop trying to turn our trio into a duo.

I replied to his message that I needed a few minutes to finish an assignment and I would be there as soon as I could. I went to the lounge at 2:25. It was technically early. Jason would be joining us any minute though and surely nothing would happen if Jason was going to be there any minute.

Adam was pacing the room when I got there. I was so in over my head. He asked about my homework. I told him. He suggested we should have dinner together before Christmas. I agreed without thinking because when he said we I assumed he meant all three of us. Then Jason walked in and Adam didn't try to set a specific day. I thought I might have just agreed to go out with Adam because I was a huge moron who had already forgotten about being careful. That was not good.

It was the week before exams and other people were using the lounge to study so we played a quiet game at the one free table. I was trying to avoid eye contact with Adam and found myself watching Jason's hands a lot. I think I probably should have realized right then why I was so intent on keeping our little group together, but as I said, I was a moron.

The next time we got together, we brought books as that seemed to be the purpose of the lounge at the end of a semester. We sat on the floor with our backs against the couch and our books and papers spread out in front of us. After a while, Adam moved to sit on the couch. Jason winked at me as it creaked under Adam's weight.

I was going to have to leave soon so I pulled out the exam schedule. I wanted to make sure we saw each other one more time to say Merry Christmas before the break. We settled on Wednesday afternoon. Adam would already be done with exams and about to pack up. Jason and I would have one more exam each on Thursday morning and then we'd leave, too.

As I tried to go back to my notes, I found I couldn't concentrate. Adam was sitting behind me on the couch and he was starting to play with my hair. He was just sort of flicking the ends of it around on the couch. I liked it, but I knew I couldn't let him do that. I was trying to delude myself into thinking that all I had to do was get through that last week without anything happening. Adam hadn't tried to follow up on his dinner invitation. I hoped that if we could just spend a few weeks apart over Christmas then everything would cool off and go back to normal… the normal that I thought I wanted.

I told both guys I was looking forward to seeing them on Wednesday and fled the lounge.

****

We hadn't talked about Christmas presents. I didn't want to be the one to bring it up because I didn't want to seem like I was fishing. That left me to fret a lot about whether or not I should bring presents to our Christmas meeting. I settled on small gifts, tokens. I knew some of the things they liked because we sometimes snacked in the lounge. I put together two small boxes and tied bows on them. Adam's box had more pretzels and chips, while I knew Jason had a sweet tooth.

I was glad I didn't show up empty-handed because I got presents. Adam gave me the complete works of Jane Austen in one book. He knew I liked to check them out at the library and now I wouldn't need to. It was very thoughtful. Jason gave me a bunch of notebooks. He knew I was picky about notebooks and he got the right kind. He also made me promise to name a character after him if I ever wrote the novel I wanted to write. I still couldn't believe I had confided in the guys, even though I had played it off as a tiny whim and not something I really really hoped I could accomplish. I loved that Jason took me seriously and that he wanted me to remember him.

And then I realized that there might be something terribly wrong. Adam and Jason hadn't gotten anything for each other. Was that a guy thing? I didn't know about guy things. I wracked my brain trying to remember if Andy had given his friends gifts in high school. I really didn't know the answer. I hoped the guys either didn't notice or didn't think it was strange. We mostly talked about our plans for the break and then we said our goodbyes. We were all smiles. Everything was good. And then it wasn't.

I had barely gotten back to my room when I got a text from Adam saying I had left something in the lounge. I wasn't sure what it was. I went right back up those stairs anyway. I walked right in. I knew as soon as I saw him that I hadn't left anything behind.

He was just standing there, waiting for me. He said, "Hi."

"Hi." I didn't say anything else. He didn't either. Not right away. I kind of thought one of us should mention that I was there under false pretenses. I was afraid that might force him to say why he had really called me back. I hoped if I kept my mouth shut that he'd chicken out.

He said, "So you liked the book, right?"

I nodded. Still not saying anything. Still hoping for chickening out.

He took a few steps forward so that he was standing right in front of me. "I just…" He swallowed hard. "I just wanted to say how much I'll miss you while we're on vacation." He reached his right hand to my left arm and brushed his fingertips up and down near my elbow. I looked at his hand on my arm for a moment. Let my eyes go past it to that orange couch. Then the big chair. I took a quick look at his face. Big mistake. Looked at the floor.

"Charlotte?" My name was barely a whisper. We both knew he was asking if it was okay to kiss me. We were both waiting for me to respond, but I didn't know how. I wanted him to kiss me and I didn't. I liked him too much and not enough at the same time.

Adam seemed encouraged by the fact that I wasn't running away. I was starting to think I should have run away. He took one more step and put his other hand up to touch my hair. "It's so soft." He said it like it was almost painful and I knew it was too late to run away. I couldn't hurt him then even though I knew I would hurt him eventually. He kissed me and it was so gentle I didn't really have to kiss him back. I did though. Just a little. Then we heard voices in the hallway and broke apart. Those people didn't come in, but the moment had ended and I was free to go.

I waved to Adam and wished him a Merry Christmas as I left the room. He looked so happy that I knew my vacation was ruined. I would spend the whole time praying that Jason wouldn't find out.

Chapter 7

I was cheered up a bit by getting to spend some time with Erin. She was very sympathetic about my problem with Adam. She had had a similar problem once and it was wonderful that the only person I could talk to about it understood so well. I tried not to dominate the conversation though. Erin had something she wanted to talk about. She had met someone. A guy who played the bass and made her wish they had rehearsals more often.

Adam called me twice during the break. It was kind of difficult. He had never called me before and I knew it was a sign that he thought things were different between us. I felt like he had screwed up a perfectly good friendship so things were different, but not in the way he thought. I didn't stay on the phone very long. It could have been worse though. I knew his parents lived only 20 minutes from mine so he could have suggested we get together. I tried to sound very busy with family stuff.

I wished Erin luck with bass guy and went back to school with my fingers crossed. I was trying really hard to imagine that things would be okay when I got there. All I could think about was the look on Adam's face after we kissed. That and the fact that I was a terrible person for letting it happen. There was always room in my head for thoughts about how I was a terrible person.

It was worse than I expected. I don't know what I expected, but what actually happened was worse. I texted the guys a meeting time almost as soon as I arrived. I hoped I didn't look overeager. They both said they could make it. That was the only good news. The 4th floor lounge was different when I entered. It was as though the actual room had changed. It had the same orange furniture and the same three round tables, but it was still different. It didn't feel like our space anymore. It just felt like a room with three people standing in it who all knew it wasn't their space anymore.

We sat down to a game and even though I had once played Risk until 3 am, I had never played a game that I wanted to end more. It dragged something awful. Adam was nudging my knee with his more incessantly than before. He kept smiling at me, and not the way he used to smile at me.

Jason didn't seem to want to look at either one of us. And after that, he responded to my next few texts only with noncommittal messages. Things about him still figuring out his new schedule.

Adam wanted to see me every day. It didn't take him long to figure out that things were not what he thought between us. He asked if he had done something wrong. I had to tell him the truth. I told him that I was the one who had done something wrong, that I should never have kissed him because I didn't…

I couldn't finish the sentence with him either. It didn't matter. He walked out and that was that. I only saw him a few more times, just passing in the halls. He always ignored me. I always deserved it.

****

I didn't know if Jason knew what had happened. I didn't know if Adam told him or he guessed or well, I didn't know. I wanted to ask him if the two of us could still be friends. That sounded to me like a conversation that 1st graders would have. So I didn't contact him at all. When I didn't hear from him for a few weeks, I assumed he didn't want to be my friend.

I tried talking to Katherine more. She didn't like to play games. She mostly wanted to talk about Caleb. She had other friends to see when she wasn't with Caleb. I think there was something going on with her, too. She just seemed frequently lost in thought and I didn't want to interrupt.

One evening near the end of January I was walking back from a shower and almost missed the studying sign. That was so not a good time for studying. Katherine had known I was in the shower. She knew I was coming back soon. I stood there holding my clothes and my bucket of soap with a towel on my head and thought about what to do. I thought about banging on the door and telling her I was coming in anyway because it was my room, too, and she had no right to leave me stranded in my pajamas with my stupid bucket of soap.

I went back to the bathroom instead. Back to the shower stalls. Each stall had two curtains, one to keep the water in and a second to give you a place to change. I reached in and turned on the water and closed the first curtain. Then I closed the curtain on my other side and sat down with my clothes in my lap. I listened to the water run and tried to remember how relaxed I had felt a few minutes ago when I had been in that water.

Small sprays of water crept under the curtain and landed on my toes. Bigger drops landed on my hands. My whole body shook from the inside out. I didn't know if I cried because Katherine had shut me out or because I had no one else to let me in. I cried until it didn't matter.

****

The relief was only temporary. It was February when I really began to go to pieces. I seemed to have forgotten how to sleep. I spent a lot of time at night separating the fringe on the edge of my blanket. I always felt tired, but sleep stayed away. I started going to bed earlier to compensate. That just gave me more time to work on the fringe. I stayed in bed longer in the mornings.

On Monday, Wednesday and Friday I had a class that started at 9:30. I started having to rush to make it. I ate my breakfast on the way. One Friday, I didn't quite finish it. I was working on the last few bites as I sat down and a chubby girl next to me said she couldn't believe I was eating that. That was a cinnamon swirl bagel. I preferred them warm with melty peanut butter on top, especially on really cold mornings like that one, but that didn't seem very portable. So it was plain. Completely plain and I couldn't figure out how it could have given offense. Since she hadn't asked a question, I opted not to say anything back at all.

But then she asked me if I got to eat breakfast every morning. That was a question. Her tone made it sound as though it was a question without a correct answer. I shrugged and stuffed the last bite into my mouth. I wanted to look as though I couldn't talk because my mouth was full and not because I didn't have a clue what she wanted me to say. She told me I made her sick before she moved to a different chair.

I made sure to finish my breakfasts after that. But sometimes I had to remind myself to eat. I was never hungry. I ate alone and rarely at the window tables. I ate at my desk whenever Katherine would let me. Once I brought back a plate of pizza for dinner and found my room was closed. I dumped it into a trash can so I could go to the computer lab.

I was spending more and more time in the computer lab. It was easy to look busy and easy to avoid conversations when I looked busy. But it wasn't a good place to cry. The shower was still a good place to cry.

It seemed that my only social interactions were at work. And that wasn't exactly social. There was more or less a script for taking orders and all my co-workers already knew I was the weird girl who didn't talk. My only chances to go off-script were with the occasional guys who asked if they could order me. I'm pretty sure they meant to be funny. I'm pretty sure they didn't intend to suggest I might be a prostitute. I usually apologized for being sold out of me. Around March I began fantasizing about coming up with a more encouraging response. But I knew I wouldn't. I knew it was just a line, just guys who thought they were clever. They weren't really trying to rescue me from my loneliness.

Erin still sent me clever texts about once a week. I think she noticed that I didn't always respond. I wasn't trying to ignore her.

Sometimes when I was crying or not sleeping I prayed to feel better. I knew I was like the blond in the joke who prays to win the lottery and never buys a ticket. It was nearly April and a Saturday when I decided to buy a ticket by visiting the lounge on the 2nd floor. I brought a book to read and sat on the couch. It was quiet. The couch was quiet. The room was quiet as well. I was the only one in there, turning the pages of my book. Sometimes I flipped forward and sometimes I flipped back. I kept getting confused on the characters because the words I read were just not staying with me.

Two girls entered the room. One had very dark skin and the other had very light hair. The one with unnaturally blond hair asked if I minded if they turned on the TV. I shook my head. I thought I didn't mind. But it was even more difficult to concentrate on my book after that. Because of the people in the lounge more than the people on the TV. The girls were chattering about the show, about the personal lives of the people on the show, about the commercials, about the shoes one of them almost bought, about the boyfriend of the roommate of someone who wasn't in the room but who should have known he wasn't a keeper, and about the shade of nail polish they were both wearing. All in what felt like an hour but was more like ten minutes.

I felt trapped. If I got up, they might think they were annoying me. I didn't want to make them feel bad. But was I annoying them by sitting there hearing their conversations even if I wasn't trying to listen? I toughed it out a few more minutes hoping it would appear that was the time I'd have left anyway.

I had an early lunch by myself in the room. Katherine was in Caleb's room. I think. Then I went back to the 2nd floor lounge. It was empty again. That was good. It felt like a minor social advantage to be there first. Something like playing on your home field, even though I was only visiting the 2nd floor. I still didn't know how I was going to make a friend without talking to anyone. I tried cards. That had worked for Adam. For a while. I brought a deck with pink polka dots on the backs and sat at a table playing solitaire. Andy had given me those cards for Christmas a few years earlier. I still didn't understand why giving me girly cards had been funny.

Three guys came in with books and notebooks. They sat at another table and didn't really notice me. I tried not to look up so they may have noticed me without saying anything and I just didn't notice them noticing. It sounded like some sort of group project. They had my sympathy. After about a half hour, I pulled out my phone and sent Erin a text because it seemed like a good idea not to look desperate for friends. It said: `It still bothers me that the dots are cut off only on one side.`

Then I switched to free cell solitaire. Too much regular solitaire might make me look boring. The guys at the other table were mostly absorbed in their project and ignoring me. But it seemed like one of them, a kind of short guy with even shorter hair, was looking at me. Just occasionally checking what I was doing. That's why I needed to display variety and contacts. I wanted to look like friend material.

I pulled out my buzzing phone and checked to see if he noticed my social interaction. He smiled. I smiled, too. Erin said: `I'm not explaining again why that's okay. Just play with the striped cards next time.`

She might have sounded irritated except that she ended it with a smiley. I actually had the striped cards in my pocket. I thought it might be a good idea to have options in case anyone offered to play with me. I heard one of the guys say that he had to go to work soon and the three of them started packing up. They stood around for a moment discussing when they'd next meet. I totally listened in. They were going to meet Tuesday afternoon and I had a class at that time. Not sure I'd have had the guts to happen to show up anyway. All three of them walked out.

I was alone in the lounge again. I thought I'd just finish my game and then maybe go to the computer lab. But then that short guy from the group project came back in. He walked over to my table and said hi before he bit his lip and looked at the ground. He looked really nervous and I thought that was wonderful. If he wasn't a talker that was one thing we had in common. I said hello and looked back at my game, trying really hard to think of something else to say. He told me he didn't know you could play free cell without a computer.

I didn't laugh. I wanted to laugh because obviously you didn't need a mouse to move cards around, but mostly because I knew it was the sort of thing that my parents would have said made them feel old. Instead I pulled out my striped deck of cards. The stripes were green so it was more masculine than my pink dots and I asked him if he wanted to try.

He sat down next to me. We played two separate and totally independent games, but we were at the same table so it felt like progress. He told me his name and I told him mine. His name was Grant. Mine was still Charlotte. There was a little bit of small talk. He was also a sophomore. I asked about the project he had been working on. He rolled his eyes at the mention of a group project, which made him seem more and more like my kind of person. But I also noticed that he apparently could *not* play free cell without a computer.

Then he realized that I was looking at my watch. I told him I was going to need to leave for work soon. He asked where I worked. Then he asked if we could try a two-player card game the next afternoon. I told him that I thought that was a good idea. He smiled and seemed less nervous. I hoped he couldn't tell I was just as nervous as when he first came in. I let him keep my striped cards until the next day. Now we had to get together. Right?

Chapter 8

We did. I saw Grant on Sunday afternoon and we played Rummy. It was a slightly different version than I played with Adam and Jason. I think it was the change in players and not in rules that bothered me. The game was more sedate. I thought Grant might be bored. But at the end of the game, he asked if I'd meet him for dinner sometime during the week. We figured out that Wednesday would work. I thought it was good that he wanted to see me again. There was hope for a relationship.

The dinner was better, somehow. He relaxed enough to tell me a funny story about one of his classes. It revolved around someone giving a stupid answer and a reference to Xena that I didn't understand. I tried to pretend I thought it was funny. But I relaxed, too. I told him how I spent a lot of time in the lounge avoiding my roommate. I didn't explain why. I just felt he should know I wasn't a freak for playing two hours of solitaire the day we met. We exchanged phone numbers and I felt like a little girl getting a friendship bracelet. But that was the high point. The low point came about 15 minutes later.

We walked out of the dining hall together. He lived on the 2nd floor and he asked me on his landing if I wanted him to walk me up to my room. I said I thought we could say goodbye just as easily on the stairs. I had said he was a little short, but I meant for a guy. I was only about an inch taller. We were pretty much eye to eye when he closed his and I realized he was moving in for a kiss. I ducked out of the way. I didn't mean to. I didn't have time to think. I didn't know it was a date. I didn't know we weren't just friends. I didn't know what to say as he mumbled an apology and ducked out the door to his floor.

I went up the stairs hoping no one would see the intense red on my face. Instead of counting the fringe that night, I spent hours trying to decide if there was any way to salvage the budding relationship. I had his number so a text seemed like my only hope. Non face-to-face contact was easier. Every message I thought of had some use of the word just and the word friends. What little I knew about guys made me think that using those words would not help the situation.

I wondered if I should try to date him. I wondered if it would be okay if I knew it was a date. I wondered if I could like him that way. I wondered if he'd even let me. Mostly I wondered why I wasn't sleeping when I was so tired.

The next day I got a text from Grant. It said: `Was it 2 soon or 2 me?`

That was my chance. He was telling me what he wanted to hear. I was scared… a little scared of ending up hurting his feelings and a lot scared of embarrassing both of us. And scared of how desperately I missed Jason. There were only a few contacts in my list after all. I saw Jason's name every time I thought about what to send to Grant, which made me think about Jason instead. I realized I needed to take what I could get. I replied to Grant: `I'll be in the lounge Saturday if you want to see me again.`

Do you want to know how long I thought about that reply before I sent it? Way too long. Most of the thought hinged around the word see. I wanted a message that could possibly be interpreted different ways. Sometimes when someone is dating someone they say they are seeing each other. Sometimes when people are angry they say they never want to see someone again. I thought I could show some remorse at having avoided the kiss and offer to date him without actually saying any of that. Because not so deep down I was still hoping he'd decide I was friend material, just friend material.

I waited until after lunch Saturday before I poked my head into the lounge. There was only one person in there. Grant was taking over the advantage that maybe I just imagined anyway. He was sitting on one end of the quiet orange couch watching golf. Yes, golf. I didn't think anyone under 70 watched golf, but that was probably because my grandfather was the only person I knew who watched golf and I didn't know that many people.

He sort of nodded as I came in and I walked rather stiff legged over to join him on the couch. I sat in the middle instead of on the other end like I wanted. I was trying. He asked me if I liked golf. I told him I didn't know because I hadn't watched much. He must have taken that to mean I didn't like it because he immediately started flipping channels.

The tension made it feel as if we were just meeting… again. I hated going backwards. It was hard enough the first time. Grant stopped his channel flipping on an old movie and looked at me questioningly. It was one of Andy's favorites so I knew when I was supposed to laugh, though I didn't think it was as funny as he did. Grant enjoyed it and I was glad that one of us was relaxing. In fact, he relaxed so much that when it ended about 40 minutes later, he was somehow sitting closer to me with one of his hands on top of my hand that was on top of my leg. I had a feeling he was about to ask me if it was still too soon. I wouldn't have told him it was if he asked, but he didn't ask. He simply made his move. I thought it wasn't so bad. I also thought I'd rather be watching TV so I was glad when other visitors to the lounge gave me an excuse to pull away.

I tried to look disappointed when I told him I should get going because I had something else to do. He didn't notice that I was vague. He suggested I visit his room on Monday when his roommate had a class. I thought that sounded like a terrible idea. I was able to answer, truthfully, that I had a class at that same time. I suggested we meet back in the lounge the next day. I would have time for a game before work. He shrugged. I left.

Sunday afternoon I brought a game I liked to call Triangle Blokus. It was actually called Blokus Trigon. Grant had never played before. He hinted that he only knew Rummy from his grandmother, and he kept trying to make illegal moves. I didn't know if I hadn't explained the rules well, which would not have surprised me, or if he hadn't been paying attention. He rolled his eyes more than once when I corrected him.

There were several people studying together at one of the other tables. As soon as they left, Grant said something mean about one of the girls before he moved over and started kissing me. I let him only for a minute before I pretended I heard someone coming and suggested he take his turn. He sighed. I don't know if you can direct a sigh at a person, but I felt like it was directed at me.

It was no surprise when I won the game. There hadn't been much competition. Grant pulled some paper out of his pocket. It was his class schedule and his roommate's. He seemed determined to get me alone. I was just as determined not to let him. I played along as we picked out a time knowing that I'd text my way out of it later.

I was distracted by thoughts of Grant during my shift at Taco Bell. And not in a good way. I was beginning to realize that I wasn't just trying to like him a certain way. I was just trying to like him. I didn't think friendship should be so trying. It only took two vague brush-offs for him to start ignoring me right back.

I didn't feel relief. I think a very small part of me wished he would have tried to make me like him. Now I had tried to make a friend and failed. I had one more person, including Adam and Beth, to add to the list of people more uncomfortable to run into than strangers. I didn't like having that kind of list. It made me hide in my room as much as Katherine would let me.

****

I skipped a few of my classes. I skipped the earliest one most. I skipped one in the afternoon once just because I wasn't paying attention to the time. And I ran out of one before it finished sometime in April because that seemed less embarrassing than bursting into tears in the middle of it.

I went to my room as soon as I got myself under control. Something was up. The whiteboard didn't say studying. It wasn't there at all. I went in. Katherine was crying. The board was on her bed. It was broken in half. She saw me looking at it and told me she didn't need it anymore. I knew what that meant, sort of. I didn't know if they had just had a fight or if they were really over. She asked if she could be alone for a while. I couldn't refuse. Not when she actually *asked* to be alone.

The computer lab was full. I didn't really want to wait in line and I had a book with me so I went up to the 4th floor lounge. I went in slowly. I wasn't ready to forgive the room for betraying me. There were three people at the closest table working on some sort of group project. I went to the next table and sat down with my book.

My phone buzzed. Erin said: `I'm watching a couple of birds out my window at the moment. I think it's the most exciting thing that has happened today.`

She was bored, too. Somehow that made me feel worse. I wished we could be bored together. Erin and I were never bored together.

I was trying to think of a good response, or just a response, when Jason walked in. He didn't really look around the room. Just sat on the couch to watch TV. I didn't think he had noticed me. I sent Erin an urgent text: `I'm in the lounge and Jason just came in. He didn't see me. What do I do?`

I held the phone tightly, waiting and watching the back of Jason's head. Erin was quick. Her reply was sloppier than usual because she knew I needed her. Grammar could be sacrificed in an emergency. She said: `Hands over eyes, guess who, requires touching?`

I figured out what she was suggesting, but I couldn't figure out why she thought touching was necessary. That felt like flirting. I liked that Jason never flirted with me. I needed a friend, not someone who would tease or confuse me. Mostly, I just desperately wanted to be near someone who felt familiar. My reply to Erin: `Here goes nothing.`

Jason was flipping through the channels as I walked over. I didn't put my hands over his eyes. I walked around the far side of the couch, sort of like on that day I first met him. He looked surprised to see me. But I think happy, too.

"Hi, Charlotte."

"Hey, mind if I sit down?"

He shook his head and said, "Of course not." I sat down at the other end of the couch and heard that now familiar creak. It was the first time that creak hadn't made me smile. I smiled at Jason anyway.

"How's your semester going?" I asked.

"Eh… can't complain I guess. How are you?"

"I'm fine," I lied. I think he knew I was lying. I don't know why I thought that.

He offered the remote. "Is there something you wanted to watch?"

I shook my head. "No, I'm just sort of killing time."

"Me, too," he said. "Needed an Ethan break."

He turned back to the TV to watch the channels change. Ethan was Jason's roommate. Jason had complained about him back when I got to hear him complain about things. Apparently, Ethan wasn't a bad guy at all, just one with some rather annoying habits. The TV landed on Family Feud. Jason cocked his head at me. "What do you think? For old times' sake?"

I nodded. I missed old times.

We watched quietly. I wanted to ask him why we needed Adam. After a minute, I noticed the people working at the table pack up and leave. We were alone. I wondered if we needed those other people, too. Would Jason leave now, too? I tried to look interested in the show, but it didn't feel like old times. I felt weird. I mean, I felt weirder than usual. I felt like Jason was watching me.

When it got to the last round, where the host asks five quick questions, Jason answered every one of them with the word chicken. He looked at me each time. I could tell he was trying to make me laugh. For question five, chicken turned out to be a good answer. He stood up and cheered. I cracked a smile.

Then the second contestant came out to answer the same five questions. Jason kept saying chicken and somehow made it sound like he was just coming up with that answer each time. He finally got to me. I laughed.

Unfortunately, it turned out that my funny bone must have been connected to my crying bone because the laugh turned into a cry before I could stop it. Jason looked startled. I was so embarrassed to be sitting there crying in front of him that it made me cry even harder.

He slid a little closer to me on the couch. "Charlotte, what's wrong?"

I shook my head and managed to say, "Nothing."

"It doesn't look like nothing, but you don't have to tell me." He sat there for a minute looking as helpless as I felt. "Wait a sec." He ran from the room, came back a minute later with a box of tissues and closed the door behind him.

He sat next to me on the couch and held out the tissues. I took a few out of the box and worked on catching my breath. He didn't say anything. He just sat there. "I'll be okay in a minute," I tried to assure him. I don't think he believed me. The TV was still on and we both pretended to watch. I don't remember what was on.

When I was sure that my face was done leaking, I tipped my head over and rested it on his shoulder. I was exhausted and he felt friendly even if we weren't really friends. I started watching his hands. He had put the tissue box down and had his hands in his lap. Every now and then, he'd rub his palms on the tops of his thighs. Then he started drumming the fingers of both hands on his legs. I thought he must have been getting bored of sitting there with me. But I felt like I could sit there forever if only he would keep his hands still. I put my left hand on top of his right to keep it from moving. His whole body froze. Oops. I hadn't meant it to be such a harsh reprimand.

Then the door opened and what seemed like a huge crowd of people came in. It was probably about seven or eight, mostly guys. One of them asked if we were watching the game. Jason shrugged and handed over the remote. I left.

Chapter 9

I entertained hopes over the next few days that Jason would contact me. I don't know why. I don't know why anyone would want to hang out with someone who dissolved into a puddle of tears for no reason. But I missed him. It was always Erin though. She was texting me nearly every day. I think even from 300 miles away she knew something was wrong.

Erin was pretty smart. I was beginning to realize that there was something wrong with me, too. I wasn't just lonely. I had always been the weird girl who never talked but I had never felt completely isolated by it. I had Erin and I had my family, even my annoying brother. School was different. There were people everywhere and I didn't feel connected to any of them. I was constantly stressed out by the presence of strangers and had no familiar outlets.

I went home that weekend for the first time since Christmas. I hadn't wanted my parents to see me because they knew me well enough to know when something was wrong. I didn't care anymore. It was worse that Jason knew.

My parents were great. They could tell something was bothering me, but didn't press me for information. They just went to work trying to make me feel better. My mom did my laundry for me. She hadn't done that since I was maybe 12 years old. At least, not without giving me a hard time about it. My dad let me watch a movie with my head on his shoulder. It was comforting in a different way than Jason's shoulder.

On Sunday, I went to church with my parents. I think they knew I only went when I was home, but they didn't say anything about that either. We made cookies together after lunch. I loved the smell of cookies baking.

I took about four dozen back to school with me and brought them up to the 4th floor lounge. There were three people in there watching TV. I asked if anyone wanted a cookie. Sometimes my voice doesn't work properly when I'm nervous. They didn't hear me over the TV. I walked around next to the TV and mentioned that I had cookies from home if anyone wanted one. That got their attention. One guy yelled something about free cookies to someone in the hallway and word spread. Soon there were at least ten of us in the room munching on cookies. A few others popped in just to grab a cookie before popping out again.

I endured the small talk like some sort of therapy for almost an hour. I didn't form any connections that day. But for a little while I was not the weird girl who didn't talk. I was the weird girl who brought cookies. I was okay with that. In fact, no one really pointed out that I was weird. Mostly people only said thank you. I was completely worn out from all the gratitude, which was a good thing because I needed to sleep.

When I got back to my room I noticed that my mother had slipped a rosary into my purse. It was the one with rainbow beads that I loved as a child and was never allowed to touch. I put it under my pillow and fingered the beads instead of my blanket fringe. I slept long and hard that night and for the next several nights. It seemed that once I remembered how to sleep, I couldn't stop. I nearly overslept for that 9:30 class on a Friday so I took my breakfast to go. It was another bagel. I ate it slowly, thinking that I wouldn't let anyone make me feel bad for having something to eat. I still finished it before I made it to class.

****

We were only two weeks from exams and the weather was starting to warm up. I went back to daily dresses. People noticed. Guys noticed. I started to get an occasional honk or whistle again. I realized I had missed the attention, sort of. I can't say I really enjoyed being honked at, but somehow, just a little bit, it was better than being ignored altogether. One guy honked at me and I decided that I wouldn't ignore him either. I smiled and waved. Then I saw brake lights.

He pulled his car into a driveway just ahead of me and waited. I guess I shouldn't have been surprised. A wave does after all mean hi. We had a perfectly nice chat though. He didn't try to hit on me. Just said he had to stop because he couldn't believe I actually waved back. He said no one ever waved back. I asked why he honked if he didn't expect a response. He couldn't answer that, but he seemed to think I was funny. Then he told me to have a nice day and I think I did.

I sent Erin a long email that included an apology for being distant. Figuratively distant anyway. No one needed to apologize for the real distance. Then I threw myself into my schoolwork. I had been zoning out in some of the classes I didn't skip and had some catching up to do. It felt good to have a focus. It felt good to be busy in the computer lab instead of just trying to look busy.

The housing forms arrived and Katherine asked me if I wanted to check the box. I did if she did. I think we both knew we weren't ever going to be friends, but we could coexist peacefully and we both thought that was better than the possible alternative. Katherine left the day before I did. I packed up my dorm room feeling relieved and disappointed at the same time. The second semester had seemed so much longer than the first. And yet, I remembered so much less of it.

My car was full and I went back one last time to make sure my room was totally empty. It was. It still looked small with nothing in it. I was ready to go. Something was holding me there. I felt like saying goodbye to the 4th floor lounge. I had only been up there once since the day I cried on Jason's shoulder. I hoped he might be in there. I hadn't looked again because I hated to be disappointed. Now I felt like one last look. Even though they were over, I wanted to remember the good times during the summer.

I smelled pizza on my way up the stairs. It seemed there was a small post-exam party happening in the lounge. I wasn't going to interrupt. I was just going to take a peek. But then I noticed that Jason was in there. I felt like maybe I should say something to him, apologize maybe or just make sure he wasn't worried about me. He was talking to someone else though so I was going to slip away. He saw me standing in the doorway and he waved.

I smiled and he came out to meet me. "Hey, Charlotte, you leaving today?"

"Any minute actually. I'm all packed."

"Big plans for the summer?"

"Yes. I plan to do nothing. Except go to work and maybe sleep in a lot."

Jason smiled. It brightened his whole face and his blue eyes sparkled like in the old days. I think that was when he relaxed, when he stopped worrying that I was some sort of crying bomb. "That sounds a lot like my summer," he said.

"Well, I hope you enjoy it." I thought I should leave. I had already told him I was packed and my car was probably blocking other people who needed to pack. I turned to go. But Jason called me back and I hope I didn't turn around too fast.

"Hey, Charlotte, can I ask you something?"

I looked up at him. I might have taken one step too many and he was at least six inches taller than me.

"Well… I was just wondering why you keep coming to the 4th floor lounge."

He rushed into an explanation and I hope it was because of my politely puzzled expression and not because I was trying to go back to having at least four feet between us.

"I mean, I know you live on the 3rd floor and there's a lounge there, but I always bump into you up here."

Oh, great. Jason had figured out that I was weird. I shrugged. "This one's just better."

He laughed. "They're exactly the same except the other one is closer to your room."

I shook my head. "No, this one is better."

"Why?" His eyes said that he wasn't just giving me a hard time. He wanted an answer to his question.

"Um… I don't know… I guess I like the noise the couch makes?"

A knowing look came over his face and yet I thought I saw a trace of disappointment. I started to walk away again. Slowly, just in case. I said, "I'll definitely be spending time in this lounge again next year." I had just decided that as I said it. I planned to reclaim it even if I had to do it alone.

But I might not have to because Jason said, "You can always let me know when you're in there."

I told him I would. On the drive home and the whole time I was unloading everything into my old bedroom, I thought about that fairly brief conversation with Jason. It had been so friendly and natural. Could we have had a similar conversation in January? Some version of it that would have meant we were still friends without Adam? I thought that if we could have, it was probably my fault that we hadn't.

Chapter 10

My summer went pretty much as I told Jason it would. I worked at a Taco Bell near my parents' house. I had worked there in high school and it was owned by the same couple as the one near school. They let me switch between them. I slept in when I could and I spent time with Erin when I could. Things hadn't worked out with the bass player. She had her sights on someone new. They had exchanged phone numbers before summer so now she had someone else to entertain with her long distance texts. She was a little disappointed in his typing. He was a bit careless with autocomplete and insisted on using the letter u in place of the word.

About a month before school started, I got a text from Jason. It simply said: `Played ping pong today and thought of you.`

I assumed he must have been playing with someone who sucked at ping pong. But then I had something of a revelation. Jason had thought about me. He had thought about me and let me know it. And that made me feel good. Well, it made me feel lousy about my ping pong skills, but it made me feel good in general. And how many times had I thought about Jason that summer?

About a million and twelve. I hadn't texted him once. Or called. Or emailed. Or driven to Indiana. I thought I should work on that if I wanted us to be friends when school started.

Except for the driving to Indiana thing. There were a lot of reasons that wasn't going to happen. Most of them perfectly normal. But just because I wasn't a talker didn't mean I couldn't communicate with people. Or at least try to communicate with people.

I didn't go nuts. I didn't want Jason to think he had said anything as encouraging as hi. I did reply to his message. I asked if the ping pong table had a hole in it. And then about a week later when I thought about him for what must have been the million and eighty-seventh time, I sat down on the couch with my phone and told myself I wasn't going to get up until I sent him a message. After more thought than I want to admit, I sent: `So how's the sleeping in going for you this summer?`

I hoped he remembered our last conversation as well as I did. I sat there nervously for a while, wondering if he'd get the message right away and if he'd have time to respond. Then my phone buzzed happily.

`Excellent.  How about you?`

Just like that. No letters pretending to be words. I was going to brag about that next time I saw Erin. I said: `Sleep is good.  How's work?`

Jason said: `Work is less good than sleep.  But I only have two more weeks.`

I said: `Does that mean you're looking forward to school?`

There was a fairly long pause. I was starting to think he had put his phone down before my last question. Then he said: `I'm looking forward to the lounge.`

I said: `Me, too.`

And then I called Erin. She was totally jealous.

I got a surprise in the mail a few days later. A new roommate assignment. I didn't know if there had been some sort of mistake. But for whatever reason, I was about to meet someone named Abigail. And then I was going to have to figure out how to live with her. But there was good news. I was moving to the 4th floor.

I looked over Abigail's contact information. There was no phone number so I was off the hook there. Just an email address. I thought about sending her a brief note. Something that said I was friendly and not weird. The thought was familiar. Futile, but familiar. When I sat down at the computer, however, I found that she had already contacted me.

Charlotte,

I got our room assignment in the mail and have been trying to decide how to introduce myself to you. I'm going to be a freshman so I don't know what someone might want to know about a future roommate. I think I'm nice and I hope we can get along. I'm trying not to bring too much stuff so I won't crowd the room, although my parents gave me a mini-fridge to take. Will that be okay? Is there anything I really should or shouldn't bring with me? I like to go to bed early, but I'm a sound sleeper so you won't have to worry about waking me up. I don't smoke. I hope you don't, but if you do that's okay. I'm excited about starting classes and also scared to death. Is that weird? One more thing, I know the form says Abigail, but no one calls me that. Please call me Abby.

Abby

There were a couple of reasons that I really liked Abby's email. The first was that I got the impression that it had taken her a long time to write it. I don't know why I thought that other than my own experiences with suffering over emails to strangers. The second reason was that she asked me questions, which gave me something to write in reply. By the time it was move-in day, we had exchanged a few more short emails. I thought I might not have to pretend to sleep when she arrived.

Abby was coming all the way from North Carolina and not expected until the evening. I thought it would be a good idea to get all my stuff arranged first so we wouldn't have to move around the tiny room at the same time. I unpacked a box and then paced for a while. I unpacked another box and then paced for a while.

It was a pretty long afternoon with lots of pacing and a small lunch. I was pretty hungry by dinnertime. That seemed like a good time to take a break. But I couldn't go to the dining hall until I cleaned up a little. I was wearing an unflattering shirt and shorts because it was move-in day and I was kind of sweaty because move-in day was in August.

I wanted to pretend the people eating dinner hadn't already seen me walking back and forth to my car in my work clothes so I changed into a clean flowery dress and stopped in the bathroom to wash my face. I made a sandwich and took it to one of those tables by the windows. I watched people carrying boxes and was glad I was done with that part of my day.

My phone buzzed shortly after I sat down. I expected something from Erin about the chore of moving in since she was moving in somewhere else the same day. I picked up my sandwich and almost ran from the room when I saw the text. It was from Jason. It said: `The lounge hasn't changed.`

My sandals tapped lightly on each stair as I tried to make my way quickly to the 4th floor. I was on the landing between the 3rd and 4th floors when I almost ran right into Jason. That would have been bad and not just because I was holding a sandwich. I hadn't thought about how desperate it might look to go running up to the lounge because of a simple text. If I hadn't met him on the stairs, I might have had time to realize that before I actually walked into the lounge. Or I could have at least ditched the food so I could pretend I had been right around the corner in my new room.

"Charlotte!" he said. He looked and smelled like he had just gotten out of a shower. "I didn't expect, um, did I interrupt your dinner?"

Was I going to say no when I was holding the evidence? I tried to think really fast. "Um… no, you *improved* my dinner."

He smiled. That must have been a good recovery.

I think I was smiling, too. I was happy to see him. I was also trying to play it cool. Not sure which emotion my mouth was following.

"So…" he said, "Are you all unpacked?"

"Mostly. I mean, it's all in my room but I have some organizing to do."

"Same here. I was just on my way to work on that some more."

"Oh, but… you're not on the 4th floor this year?"

He shook his head. "2nd."

"Then what were you doing in the 4th floor lounge? I thought you said it was strange to visit a lounge that was not on your floor."

"Um…" Jason looked confused for a few seconds and then I think he remembered the conversation. "I think I said it was strange when *you* did it."

"Oh… well, either way, I hope you won't be expecting me to hang out in the inferior 2nd floor lounge this year just because it's closer to you now."

He laughed. "It's not inferior. It's exactly the same."

"I disagree." I hoped Jason was laughing at my stubbornness and not… well, I could think of any number of reasons he might be laughing at me and all of them were less flattering than being stubborn. So I was hoping it was stubbornness as a group of three guys walked past us up the stairs. We moved aside to make room for them and the last guy in the line leaned in and whispered to me as he passed. I ignored him, but I think I blushed a little because Jason did not.

"What did he just say to you?"

"Nothing." I answered reflexively because I didn't want to say it, but we both knew that was a lie so I corrected myself. "I mean nothing important."

Jason looked upset, almost angry. I didn't know if it was because of the guy or because I wouldn't tell him what he had said. I didn't want Jason to be angry with me so I told him that the guy had said, "I'd treat you better than dinner in a stairwell, honey." Except I left off the honey.

"That wasn't very nice."

"It doesn't matter. He was just being stupid and he's gone." Jason still looked upset, but he didn't say anything and I didn't know how to make things better when I hadn't done anything. "Look," I said, "I'd rather eat my dinner in a stairwell with a friend than do anything with that jerk and that's why I don't care what he has to say."

Jason looked appeased, but not entirely happy. "Fine. I'll drop it," he said.

I took a bite of the sandwich I had forgotten I was holding to show how much I didn't mind eating on the stairs. But then I said I had to go because I was expecting my new roommate soon and wanted to clean up a bit more before she got there. Jason said he'd see me soon as we headed in opposite directions on the stairs. I hoped he meant that. I know some people just say that as a farewell, but I didn't think Jason would tease me like that. I felt like we had gotten off to a good start, despite the interruption, and maybe we could be real friends that year. The thought made me a little braver for meeting Abby.

She arrived a little after 7 pm, parents and 16-year-old sister in tow. Abby was barely 5 feet tall and though she wasn't pudgy, she had a very round face. Her dark brown hair was cut in angled layers above her shoulders. I wondered if that was an attempt to make her face appear less round. I didn't know anything about that sort of thing. I just knew it was a much more complicated haircut than I had ever had. Or given.

Both of her parents shook my hand as they introduced themselves. I offered to help unload the car and they thought I was really sweet. Her mom stayed at the car and handed out boxes to the rest of us. She saved the heavy ones for Abby's dad and the questions for me. Every time I went to collect a box I had to reveal a little factoid about myself. My age, my major, my hometown. Did I have brothers or sisters.

I was rewarded each time with similar information about Abby. Most of this she had already told me in her emails. The most important thing I learned from the exchange was that Abby had apparently not shared the contents of those notes with her mom. Abby was a private person. Perhaps not a talker.

Her parents left for their hotel as soon as the car was empty. They were going to spend Tuesday with Abby and then drive back on Wednesday. I turned on the TV as soon as Abby and I were alone in the room. I think she was relieved. For an hour or so, I sort of watched TV and sort of watched her unpack while she sort of unpacked and sort of watched TV. Then she said the rest could wait until later. I went to take a shower and Abby was in bed when I got back. She might have been pretending to sleep.

Chapter 11

Abby was up before me in the morning and already gone. Her parents must have picked her up early.

I went to the bookstore right after breakfast and then spent most of the day alone in my room. I organized my stuff a little better and surreptitiously looked over Abby's things. The room was exactly the same as the one I had shared with Katherine. It looked and felt so completely different when filled with someone else's belongings.

Thinking of Katherine made me pull out the student directory. I had no intention of calling her. I was just curious where she had ended up. If I might run into her, I probably needed to think of something to say. What if she had asked not to room with me after all? What if she thought I had? But I couldn't find her in the directory. She had either dropped out or transferred. I wasn't sure how I felt about that. But I didn't feel anything about it for very long. I felt hungry instead.

I walked to the dining hall intending to bring dinner back to the desk in my room. While I was picking out my food, however, I realized that I had said thank you to the clerk in the bookstore. That was it. Those were the only two words I had spoken to anyone all day. I thought of the previous semester and panicked. I think it was panic. It must have been something completely irrational because that's the only way I can explain what happened next.

I took my slice of pizza out to the tables and looked around the room. I thought maybe there was a freshman who didn't know anyone either and I could do a few minutes of small talk. There was a whole table full of guys nearby and they noticed me looking.

One of them yelled out, "Hey, you can sit with us!"

Another one added, "Yeah, there's plenty of room."

I took the last empty place at their table, not quite believing what I was doing. I sat down and said, "Hi. I'm Charlotte."

At least one of the guys appeared surprised that I had actually joined them. The one who had called me over, who seemed to be the ringleader of sorts, was nothing but pleased with himself. "I'm Dan," he said. "You a freshman?"

"Junior," I corrected. He nodded his approval. "What about you?" I asked, glancing around the table in an attempt to make that a collective you.

Dan answered for the whole group. "We're all new except for Michael. He's a sophomore." Dan gestured to a red-haired guy next to him. He had actual red hair.

Michael nodded and said, "Yeah, I was here last year, but I don't remember you from last year. I think I'd remember *you.*" He kind of looked me up and down as he said it.

I looked him right in the eye for like two whole seconds and said, "Not if I didn't want you to." I don't think he knew what I meant by that, but he laughed anyway. I didn't know what I meant either.

One of the other guys spoke up next and asked if I had a boyfriend. I tried to sound very casual as I said, "Not at the moment."

There was a general "ah" around the table as though I had just asked for resumes. That must have been what Dan thought anyway because he went around the table giving a description of my choices. "Well, you know Michael here is a sophomore. He's a business major. That's Keith. He's undecided. Likes basketball. David's going to study computer science. Josh is from Pennsylvania. And then there's me. I'm eighteen, graduated in the top 10% of my class, and I'm very *very* sensitive." He looked serious and blinked his eyes at me a few times.

I had to laugh at the sales pitch. Michael elbowed him. "Come on, man. You're not giving the rest of us a chance."

"Don't worry, you all have a chance." I don't know what made me say that. I'm pretty sure I had never flirted with anyone in my life. Not intentionally. I was sure I'd be bad at it. But the guys smiled and started slapping each other's hands so I think it was okay. Then someone, I think it was Keith, asked what I was looking for in a guy.

"Hmmm…" I tried to look thoughtful. "Sensitive is good."

Dan pumped his fist.

"But I've always been partial to guys with dark hair."

Dan was a blond. He hung his head while a couple of the other guys cheered. I couldn't really think of anything else to say. The truth was that I didn't know what I wanted in a guy. I didn't have enough experience to know what was good and what was bad. I thought maybe I should think about how to get a guy I wanted after I figured out how to make friends. But I couldn't think about either at the moment. I needed to concentrate to keep up with so much conversation. The guys asked me lots of questions about the dorm and about the campus. I couldn't answer all their questions, but I smiled a lot and they seemed to think most of what I said was funny. I knew it wasn't. Maybe I was just better at flirting than I thought.

When everyone was done eating and I stood up to leave, a couple of the guys pulled out their phones and insisted I give up my number. I told them I didn't think they could be trusted with such delicate information. That was the funniest thing I had said so far.

It seemed like they gave up kind of easily on the phone thing. But then they paraded after me as I started toward my room. That seemed like a problem. I led them on a tour of the entire building. They knew what I was doing and insisted they could outlast me. Keith bragged that he had run cross country all four years of high school so there was no way I could wear him out, which prompted plenty of jokes about other ways I might be able to make the guys tired. I wished they hadn't gone there. I wouldn't let them make me blush though. I led them up and down stairs and through all three lounges. We were starting to get looks so I ducked into a girls' bathroom. They waited outside calling my name, loudly.

I gave up. I went back to my room with all five of them still following me. That was great. Now a bunch of guys who thought I liked to flirt knew where I lived. I thought I might be in big trouble.

****

I found out that Abby had picked her college, at least in part, because she had grandparents in town. They picked her up on Friday so she could spend the weekend with them. She spent a lot of time in the room during the week and I thought we were starting the year just fine. She left me alone and I left her alone. She definitely was not a talker. At least, not in the traditional sense. There were a lot of times I caught her mumbling to herself. Abby was kind of weird. I kind of liked that.

My first few classes went pretty well. But then on my first Monday, not even quite a whole week into the year, something terrible happened. The class was British Literature. The professor seemed wonderful. He did most of the talking and expected us to sit and take notes, or at least look like we were taking notes, and I thought it might just be my favorite class of the semester. On that Monday, he said it was time for our first essay. I could do that. He said we were to pick any British author we liked and compare and contrast two of his or her works in 2000 words. No problem. Compare and contrast. It was like going back to 9th grade English and with my favorite author along for the ride.

But then the professor said two words that changed everything. He said two words that made me break out in a cold sweat and forced my heart to come to a screeching halt inside my chest.

He said group project.

He said it would be a fun way to get to know each other.

At first I thought maybe I imagined he had said those things. That would have made more sense because writing is not a group activity. That was part of the reason that I was an English major. Writing isn't like talking. It only needs one person.

But then, why was everyone around me turning to their neighbors in an attempt to break into groups?

Oh, horrors!

Now I needed to sit there and look like I wanted someone to invite me into their group even though I didn't because no one wants someone in their group who doesn't want to be in their group but I really didn't want to write a paper in a group even though I needed to do just that and I didn't know how to look like I wasn't thinking that the professor I thought was nice had just turned out to be a sadist.

The traitorous professor had specified groups of three or four so two girls nearby thought they needed me. I nodded at them. I would survive this if I had to. Then a guy invited himself to join us. No one argued with him. We arranged to meet after dinner that night in a computer lab to get started. I can't tell you how much I was looking forward to it.

I had just a few minutes to kill between that class and the next one so I turned on my phone thinking I'd send Erin a message. But I already had one from Jason. It said: `Can you meet me in the lounge at seven?`

Nuts. That was exactly when I was supposed to be having fun getting to know my new classmates. I replied: `Sorry. Nightmare group project. I'll let you know when it's over.`

I realized I was too distraught to send Erin a witty text. Instead I sent: `Formerly good prof is trying to ruin my life. I'll tell you all the gory details later.`

Then I went to my next class and waited for the room to fill.

I ate dinner in my room. Abby had a 6 o'clock class and that seemed like a reasonable time for dinner. I walked two buildings over to the computer lab where I was supposed to meet my new group at 7 pm. That was so not a reasonable time for a group project. I would rather have walked to school barefoot in the snow than do a group project once I got there.

One of the other girls was walking in the same time I was. She had short blond hair and an orange shirt. We saw the third girl, who was wearing a baseball cap with a brown ponytail sticking out the back, near a computer and we joined her.

Baseball cap girl said, "So I think we should do Jane Austen."

I liked baseball cap girl. I didn't say anything right away though. I wanted to see how orange shirt girl would respond.

She said, "Well, that might be easy, but don't you think everyone is going to do Jane Austen?"

"So what?" Baseball cap girl shrugged. "As long as we write a good paper, it doesn't matter what anyone else does."

Orange shirt girl didn't look convinced. Then the guy for our group came in. He was taller than I remembered. Of course, he had been sitting down in class. Orange shirt girl explained the ideas and he sided with her. Then all three of them took turns throwing out different authors' names to see which ones we had read. I mostly nodded or shook my head as they looked to see if I'd be able to contribute. 45 minutes later we had decided on our topic author: Jane Austen.

Tall guy jumped in front of a computer and created a document. Baseball cap girl commented that it was just like a guy to assume he got to drive. He typed out an opening sentence that nobody liked. Orange shirt girl thought maybe we should write out a list of similarities and differences first.

That was probably a good idea. We were still doing that when we realized that it was 10 pm and the computer lab was closing. We planned to meet again on Wednesday.

Wednesday wasn't any better. We printed out the list of ideas and tall guy sat at the computer while we tried to organize the thoughts of four people into one paper. Tall guy had only read one of the books we were using. We wrote 423 words that day in another three hours.

By the third day orange shirt girl, whose name was Briana, figured out that I was not a talker. She said that I needed to contribute more so it was my turn to type. I didn't argue.

I sat there while they discussed what to tell me to write. Briana dictated a sentence to me and I wrote it out. Then I added a second sentence to stretch out the thought because I was starting to think we'd never finish the paper.

"Um, yeah, that will work," Tall guy said.

"No, we don't need that," baseball cap girl said.

Delete.

"Wait, put that back in." That was Briana.

Baseball cap girl argued, "But we already mentioned the fathers. We should move on to another point."

"We have to write 2000 words."

"We already have 1000."

"Yes, 1000. We need 2000. We should keep that sentence. It's the only thing Charlotte has contributed."

Ouch. I was sitting right there.

"Fine. Keep it."

Tall guy had let them argue. Now that the sentence was back in, he said, "I thought it was a good thought, Charlotte."

I internally thanked tall guy for his pity. But I was being sarcastic.

We got to 1417 words before we were again kicked out of the computer lab and again picked out another time to meet. That would be Monday evening again. We'd be a week from the due date and more than half done. Baseball cap girl was sure we'd finish in one more meeting. Briana thought we'd made some excellent progress. Tall guy conceded that he'd have waited till the night before it was due if we weren't in a group. I smiled and thanked everyone for their help. All were simple statements. And all were clearly forced. I knew none of them would ever talk to me again when the project was finished. Unless of course we got stuck together for another one. I tried not to think about that.

Tall guy walked out of the lab with me and asked where I was headed. Then he offered to walk me back since it was getting late. I told him not to bother. There were lots of lights and it was only two buildings over. He said he'd see me in class then and turned to go in a different direction.

Abby was gone when I got back to the room. I assumed her grandparents had picked her up for the weekend again. I had to work on Saturday, but otherwise spent most of the weekend alone in my room.

Chapter 12

The guys who knew where I lived turned out to be pretty harmless. I had brought my own whiteboard to school. I thought it might be nice to get a message other than studying. Nearly every day, I'd get a message from one or more of those guys. Usually something along the lines of "Charlotte, we miss you!" or "Charlotte, you can't hide from us forever." I figured they'd get tired of it eventually.

Monday came very fast. In class that morning, Briana instructed all three of us to be thinking about the project so we could definitely finish that evening. She clearly felt like she was doing the bulk of the work. She gave me a fierce look during these instructions. I thought maybe she should have been looking at the professor like that.

Baseball cap girl got to the computer lab before me that evening.

"Hey, Charlotte," she said.

"Hi. Are you ready to finish this paper?"

She rolled her eyes. I think that meant she was as ready as I was. Then she leaned in a bit, like she was about to tell me a secret. "I want to tell you something."

"Okay?"

"I think Ryan is going to ask you out and Briana wants to go out with him so I think you should tell him no unless you really like him, too."

I said, "What?"

It was kind of a stupid thing to say because I had heard her just fine. And what she said made sense. If you knew that tall guy's name was Ryan. I was just surprised to find out how naïve I was. I had thought all the drama in our group was coming from the fact that writing was not a group activity.

"Do you like him?" she asked me.

I shook my head. It was a reflex. I hadn't really thought about Ryan that way. I was just trying to survive until the paper was finished. Baseball cap girl leaned back and nodded toward the entrance. Briana was walking in with Ryan. Briana looked at me with something like disgust. "Why are you wearing a dress again?"

It was the same dress I had worn to class that morning. I thought it would have been weirder to change in the middle of the day. I just shrugged.

"Are you trying to impress someone?"

"I just like this dress."

She laughed. It wasn't a nice laugh. It was the way you'd laugh at a four-year-old wearing a superhero costume three weeks after Halloween.

I sat down. "Can we please get this over with?"

"If you'd help." Briana said it under her breath, but we all heard her. The tension didn't help anything. We read through what we had written so far and began to discuss what we could add.

Slowly…

Horribly slowly…

We added sentences here and there.

At 9:45 we needed 200 more words. I was not returning to that computer lab a fourth time for a paper I could have written in two hours by myself. I backed up and added a few lines to a paragraph I thought was short.

Briana said, "Don't you think you should check with us first?"

"Do you want me to delete it?"

Briana looked torn. Ryan and baseball cap girl said no together.

I added a few more lines and no one said anything. Two sentences for a conclusion. Now we had 2030 words. I went back to the beginning so we could all read it through together. Briana insisted on a pair of minor rewordings. I say insisted even though she didn't get any resistance because both of her suggestions were completely unnecessary. But we were done.

I stood up slowly and fiddled with my purse a bit. The other three had been standing behind me and I hoped they'd leave quickly so I could walk out in peace. Baseball cap girl waved and practically ran to the exit. I'd have done that if I hadn't been blocked in. And if I hadn't been in on the secret, I probably would have thought I imagined that Ryan and Briana were leaving as slowly as I was. Instead I got the impression that Ryan was waiting for me and Briana was waiting for Ryan.

We moved toward the exit in silence. Briana got to the door first. She turned to Ryan as she used her back to open the door. "You live this way, right?" She nodded her head to the left. Obviously the direction she was going.

I tried to slip quickly out the door next to her to move to the right.

I heard Ryan say, "Yeah, but go ahead," a few seconds before he was walking next to me. Then he said, "I thought if I just escorted you without asking you wouldn't have to refuse out of politeness. It is dark."

"Okay." I figured that since I didn't have a choice in the matter that I might as well say okay. I didn't say that I hadn't refused out of politeness. I had refused because Ryan was just as scary to me as anyone who might be lurking in the bushes. Not that he had said or done anything to make me think he might be some kind of criminal. I just figured the odds of me being confronted by a guy in the bushes were so low as to be almost nonexistent. There weren't any bushes and there were a few other random people here and there on the sidewalks. But the odds of me being confronted by Ryan now seemed nearly 100%. I preferred my chances with hiding in the bushes guy. But I said okay anyway.

Ryan said, "Glad we're done with that project, huh?"

I nodded.

"Um, the class seems okay otherwise though?"

That was a statement, but he said it like a question so I thought I should agree. "Yeah… I've had professors who were more boring."

Ryan laughed. That was bad. I wasn't funny.

He didn't say anything for a moment and then he said, "By the way, I like your dress, too."

I didn't know what to say to that. I thought reminding me of the unpleasantness with Briana wasn't his best move. But it was still a compliment. I hate to admit how old I was when I finally figured out that thank you was always the best and simplest response to a compliment. Instead I told him that I just got it over the summer. Then there were a few more moments of silence.

We were nearly to the door of my building so I knew that if he was going to do what baseball cap girl thought he was going to do then he would need to do it soon. Which meant I needed to think fast. Did I want to go out with Ryan if he asked me? That was sort of complicated. Or at least I was making it complicated in my head.

I didn't really want to date Ryan. He was very tall and I had already heard a few words from his mouth that I didn't use and that I didn't care to hear. But I kind of just wanted the experience of a date. I was very inexperienced in that area. I had been on exactly three and a half dates before Grant. I was still a little confused as to how much of my time with Grant could be called dates. The other three and a half were with the same guy. It was the summer between high school and college. We met at a fast food place, not the Taco Bell where I worked, which I counted as half a date. Then we went out three more times before he gave up on me. That was the one guy I had kissed before Adam. I hadn't let him do anything but kiss me and that was why he gave up on me. Erin said that it was his loss and I knew she was right.

It still hurt.

I liked the idea that I could go out with Ryan once and probably not get hurt. And Briana had been mean to me and she liked him. But was I that juvenile?

Ryan reached for the door and looked like he was going to open it for me. Instead, he held it closed and turned to me. "So I was thinking," he said, "that maybe you and I could get together somewhere other than the computer lab. Maybe at the Student Union for dinner. How about Friday?"

"I…" I looked at the sidewalk. "Um, I don't think so. Maybe I'll just see you in class."

Ryan shrugged and opened the door for me. "Good night then," he said.

I mumbled a goodnight as I hurried inside. By the way, I think I was that juvenile. But I was also spineless. I had to see Ryan and Briana in class the rest of the semester after all.

****

I was sitting in an afternoon class thinking about Jason. Instead of paying attention. I probably should have been paying attention. I was thinking about Jason because I was now about three weeks into the school year and it had been about three weeks since I had seen him or even heard from him. That seemed like a bad way for us to really be friends. And I needed a friend. Despite the persistent messages on my door, which I sometimes even answered with things like "Yes, I can," I wasn't doing anything social. Abby was continuing to spend her weekends with her grandparents and we mostly ignored each other the rest of the time.

I didn't need the 4th floor lounge with such an agreeable roommate. I still peeked in there sometimes when I walked by. I knew I was hoping to find Jason in there. That seemed easier than coming out and telling him I wanted to see him. I worried that he might agree out of obligation, not friendship. Or worse, maybe he didn't want to see me at all.

Actually, I wasn't sure which of those would be worse.

It seemed that Jason and I had started the year okay. I know I looked kind of like a little kid running up the stairs to meet him. But then he asked me to meet him in the lounge. That had been a good sign. And I told him about the group project. Did that make it my turn? Was he waiting for me to suggest we get together or glad he was off the hook?

I wondered if my school offered a class on making friends. I'd probably be too embarrassed to sign up for it. People thinking I was weird because I liked to be alone was one thing, people thinking I was alone because I was weird was something else.

My classmates were beginning to stand up. Apparently the class had ended. I really should have been paying attention. I noticed that a lot of my classmates were pulling out their phones as they left. I wondered how many of them would have messages from friends. The thought spurred me to action. I pulled out my own phone and gathered some determination. I texted Jason: `Want to meet for dinner somewhere other than a stairwell?`

I hope he wasn't in class because he responded right away with: `Where?`

I said: `Dining hall?`

Jason said: `Time?`

I said: `Six?`

He said: `Okay. Mind if my brother comes?`

Jason had a brother? At school!? I think Jason had mentioned a brother a few times when we had been hanging out in the lounge, but I guess I had never asked about him. Now I was curious. And more scared than I was just arranging a meeting with Jason. But I took a deep breath and typed: `Okay. See you then.`

Then I walked back to my dorm wishing I'd suggested an earlier time because I couldn't wait.

****

I got to the dining hall about fifteen minutes early. I wasn't being overeager. I was being practical. We hadn't established exactly where in the dining hall we were going to meet and I thought it was best if I waited near the doorway so we wouldn't miss each other.

I nervously smoothed the sides of my blue dress while avoiding eye contact with other people on their way to dinner. I didn't have to be social with them since I had a friend coming. A friend and someone new to meet. I might not have to be social again for at least a week. Then I saw Jason coming down the hall with a guy I knew right away was his brother. He was a bit shorter than Jason and had darker hair, but there was a strong family resemblance.

Jason introduced me to his brother, whose name was Matt, and we went in together, grabbed some food and found a place to sit.

We ate in silence for a minute or two. It wasn't the awkward silence where no one knows what to say though. I think we were all just hungry. I definitely should have suggested an earlier time.

Matt spoke first. "Jason told me you were an English major."

"That's right. I still am."

"Do you like it?"

"Most of the time."

"You probably have to write a lot, don't you?"

I nodded. I had taken a bite.

He shook his head. "I couldn't do that. I'm not a fan of writing."

"I like to write as long as I can do it by myself." I shuddered a bit at the memory of the group paper. It was a little too soon to talk about that so I asked Matt what he was studying.

"C.S. like Jason."

I nodded at both of them. That seemed like a good, practical course of study. I still wasn't sure what I was going to do with an English degree once I had one. I asked Matt how he liked school in general so far.

"Oh, it's so much better than high school. I like the breaks between classes and I don't know, it just feels like you have a little more control over your life. But I do miss having my own room." He playfully punched his brother in the arm.

"Oh, you guys are roommates?" I was looking at Jason so he answered.

"Well, apparently Ethan thought I was the annoying one and I figured Matt here was better than playing the lottery. The devil you know, right?"

"Hey!" Matt punched him again, a little harder.

"What happened to Katherine anyway?" Jason asked.

"I'm not sure actually. I'm thinking she dropped out." I was about to explain how I thought we were going to be roommates and then couldn't find her in the directory when we were interrupted by someone calling my name. Dan and Keith had spotted me and were approaching the table. I closed my eyes for a second and tried to prepare myself.

"Charlotte!" Dan said again. There was no need for him to shout. He was standing right next to me. Not that I preferred shouting across a room. "How much longer are you going to ignore us?"

"I'm not ignoring you. I wrote never, didn't I?"

"Oh!" Dan put his hand over his heart. "That hurts, Charlotte. Don't you know how much we miss you?"

I said, "I know, but go miss me over there for now."

They began to walk away with Dan calling over his shoulder, "For now! But I know you'll come around eventually."

After the interruption, Jason looked at me funny and said, "What was that all about?"

I shrugged. "I sort of accidentally got a fan club."

Matt said, "A fan club?"

And Jason said, "Accidentally?"

I shrugged again. I was way too embarrassed to explain what had happened.

"Is that who's been writing on your door?" Jason wanted to know.

"Yeah, they'll get bored of it eventually."

"Not if you keep encouraging them."

"I'm not encouraging them."

Jason snorted. He didn't believe me. I looked at Matt. He put his hands up to show that he wasn't getting involved. I didn't argue. Soon the guys would stop and it wouldn't matter whether or not Jason had believed me. But I had to admit that a tiny piece of me didn't want them to stop so maybe Jason was right and I just didn't know it.

Chapter 13

I got a text from Erin that said: `I put acid on all the rocks just for fun.`

She was taking a geology class and I suspected that was what she was talking about. It was Friday and I had just finished my last class so I called her to find out for sure and to ask about her weekend. She was about to have her second date with the guy whose texts disappointed her. She didn't seem to be finding anything else about him disappointing. I was hopeful for her. She asked if I had any plans. I told her I was going to try to get together with Jason and Matt. It had been four days since we had dinner together and I figured it was about time Matt was introduced to the 4th floor lounge. He seemed nice. I thought he could handle it.

I was still on the phone with Erin when I got to my door so she got to hear my reaction to the surprise that was waiting for me. There was a very different sort of message on my door. It said: One of us is for real now. If he asked, would you go out with him?

Erin thought I should definitely go for it. I had to think about it. Would I go out with him? Go out with whom? I didn't know which of the guys wanted to ask and I didn't really know any of them. Someone once told me though that you go out with someone to get to know him. I started to think it might be okay. It helped that Erin was working very hard to talk me into it. There weren't any friendships at stake and they weren't in any of my classes. I could just… see what happened. I wrote maybe.

Then I went into my room and texted Jason to see when he and Matt could meet me in the lounge. I hoped I wasn't pushing my luck by asking twice in a row. He didn't reply right away but we eventually set something up for Saturday. They brought that *David & Goliath* game with them. Matt was pretty good at it, too. I lost spectacularly. Twice. It was still fun. Sometimes it's harder to lose a game when you're close. You know, when you think you have a chance.

The next Friday I woke up to find a new message on my board. It said: Please meet me by the front doors at 12:30. We'll just take a walk.

I couldn't say maybe to that. After nearly a week I was starting to think he had changed his mind. Whoever he was. I was still trying to decide if that should make me feel relieved or offended. Now I was just really nervous. I wrote okay and went to breakfast. He couldn't have picked a better time. I had a class at 1 o'clock. I could find out who it was, talk for just a few minutes, and then have an excuse to leave. That wouldn't be so bad.

I had classes at 9:30 and 10:30. That didn't leave a lot of time in the morning for me to worry about the walk. I had a small lunch because my stomach was fluttering uncomfortably. Then I put my book bag over my shoulder and walked slowly toward the front doors. I considered leaving the bag so I'd have to abandon my mystery date even sooner. But that might have been either rude or cowardly. I could give this guy the full 20 minutes just to see what happened.

It was Keith. He was waiting for me and not looking all that nervous, which made me feel better and worse. He didn't look like I had the power to hurt him and that was both reassuring and threatening. I thought I should tell him the time constraint up front. "I have a class at one so we have to end up at the pointy blue building a little before that. Okay?"

Keith said, "I may be a freshman, but I've figured out the names of the buildings."

I hadn't said that for his benefit so his response made me chuckle. "Oh, I wasn't trying to be insulting. I just like to call it the pointy blue building."

Now Keith laughed. "You're kinda weird. Aren't you, Charlotte?"

I shrugged. That wasn't news to me.

We walked around a bit and ended up at the right building just in time. He asked if we could try a real date. The walk seemed very quick so I agreed to dinner the following Saturday. That wouldn't be so bad. I let him have my phone number. I didn't want to. But I was pretty sure I couldn't agree to a date and not a phone number exchange, not without being more than kinda weird.

****

I played *Carcassonne* with Jason and Matt on Tuesday. It was a game I had brought from home and neither of them had played before. It wasn't going well for them. That was mostly my fault. I'm not very good at teaching board games.

"Oh, wait," Matt said. "I think I see how the farms are coming together."

Jason was studying the board, too. "Yeah, we're going to have to play this again once I figure it out."

"I told you guys you should have read the instructions."

Matt said, "I think maybe she explained poorly on purpose to make up for the *David & Goliath* fiasco."

Jason looked at me accusingly and his eyes danced. "Charlotte! You wouldn't do that, would you?"

I just laughed. I really did tell them to read the instructions.

"Does that mean you'll at least agree to a rematch?" Jason asked.

"Sure. When?" I was always eager to set up another meeting and always happy to have someone else suggest it.

"How about after dinner Saturday. Like 6:30 or 7?"

"I can't." I wasn't sure how much time to allow for what Keith had called a real date.

"Sunday night then?"

"No, I have to work."

Jason crumpled his eyes at me. "But you never work Saturday *and* Sunday."

He was right and I could tell he knew that. I only worked two shifts a week during school and never both weekend days. My bosses were very generous with my time because I had worked for them longer than almost everyone else.

"I didn't say I had to work on Saturday. I just have something else going on." I wasn't going to tell them what it was. Not after Jason had accused me of encouraging those guys. But something about the fact that I didn't tell made them guess.

Matt said, "Oooh… Charlotte has a hot date this weekend."

Jason didn't say anything. He was watching me for confirmation. I think I confirmed it by looking like I didn't want to. Fortunately, they respected that I didn't want to talk about it and Matt went back to giving me a hard time about my game instructions. Jason was very quiet for the rest of the game. I think he was concentrating. He was the furthest behind.

****

Saturday arrived and I spent nearly an hour on the phone with Erin. That was a very long conversation for us. I wanted to know how I had let her talk me into going on a date with Keith. She said she couldn't be held responsible because she had only talked me into the first one and I had agreed to the second on my own. Then we argued over and over about whether or not a 20 minute walk could count as a date. And whether or not it mattered.

Keith and I walked to a restaurant just off campus. We ate. We talked a little. I mostly listened. Dan had said one of the guys liked basketball. I couldn't remember which one it had been, but after spending an hour with Keith I would not have guessed anyone else. And he just seemed so young. I know that sounds silly when he was only two years behind me. But he talked about high school a lot. For me, that was already starting to feel like a long time ago.

I wouldn't say the date was awful. It was not great though. I'm pretty sure Keith knew as well as I did that there was no spark. But that didn't stop him from kissing me goodnight. Stuck his tongue so far into my mouth I thought he might be checking to see if I still had my wisdom teeth. He wasn't going to find any and I didn't let him look very long.

He called me two days later to ask me out again. I don't think he was surprised when I said no. If I hurt him at all, it was his ego and not his feelings. I gave myself permission not to feel like a terrible person.

****

The following Friday I still hadn't heard from Jason (or Matt who had my number now, too) about that *Carcassonne* rematch I owed them. I sent Jason a message that said: `I have time for a rematch tomorrow if you do.`

His eventual reply: `I have a ton of homework this weekend, but we can do it soon.`

The ambiguity worried me. The only other time Jason had rejected an offer without a specific counteroffer had been when things got messy with Adam. Did he think I would ditch him if I started dating someone? I didn't know what was going on. I thought I'd work on telling myself to relax for a few days just in case he really did have some big project due. Maybe it was a group project. I could understand his distraction. The next Friday I was still working on telling myself to relax and it still wasn't working.

Then I got a text from Matt asking how I was doing. That was it. It just said: `Hi, Charlotte. How are you?`

How in the world was I supposed to answer that!? How was I? I was fine except that I thought I was becoming friends with these two guys and now they seemed to have deserted me for no reason. Obviously, I couldn't say anything like that. I'd look needy. I'd look like I didn't have other friends to distract me.

I slipped the phone back into my purse because I was going to need to think about how to reply. I was walking back from my last class and trying to calm down enough to enjoy the weather. It was nearly Halloween and unusual to have a light sweater kind of day so late in the year. The semi-warmth had drawn people out to the lawns and I looked around at some of them. People were reading books propped against trees. Some were standing around talking. There seemed to be a big group in the distance playing football, or something that looked like football to my untrained eye. Right in front of my dorm were two guys playing Frisbee, outdoor Frisbee. I realized that they looked familiar. Maybe I could stop fretting over how to reply to Matt's text now.

I watched for a while and then they noticed me watching. Matt waved and started jogging over. He was farther so Jason walked and they got up to me at about the same time.

"Hey, Charlotte. Did you get my text?"

"Not yet," I lied. "Is it important?"

"No, just checking in."

"Okay. Well, I'm fine. How about you guys?"

"Sure. Are you loving this weather or what?"

"It's great. Probably too nice to do any indoor games, but if you guys wait much longer to try *Carcassonne* again then I'm just gonna have to teach it to you all over again."

Matt smiled and elbowed his brother, who so far hadn't said anything. "We wouldn't want that now. Would we, Jason?"

"I guess not. Do you think we can squeeze it in this weekend?"

I nodded. "I'm free all day Saturday."

Matt raised his eyebrows at me. "No dates?"

"There was just the one." I think I had convinced Erin that the walk didn't count. And Jason and Matt didn't know about that anyway. I must have sounded a little defensive because Matt dropped it right away.

"Okay," he said. "*Carcassonne* tomorrow. And right now you can play Frisbee with us."

"No, thanks. I'll just watch."

"Come on, Charlotte."

"No… really, I'll just watch."

Jason started laughing. "I don't think you're going to have any luck, Matt. Charlotte has some sort of moral objection to Frisbees."

"I do not. I just… I'm not coordinated enough to catch anything."

"Oh, then you can just throw." Matt tried to hand the Frisbee to me.

I refused to take it. "I can't throw either."

"Yeah, you can. Everyone can throw a Frisbee."

"Trust me. I can't."

"I'm sure you can."

"I'm sure I cannot."

Matt wrinkled his forehead at me. "I don't believe you. Why don't you want to throw it?"

"Because I can't."

"Here…" He held out the Frisbee again. "Just try it once to see how easy it is."

"Fine." I put down my bag. At that point I was less concerned about looking foolish trying to do something I couldn't than I was in *proving* that I was right about not being able to do it. I took the Frisbee and looked at Matt, waiting for some guidance.

He started jogging backwards as he said, "All right. Jason, you show her how and I'll go catch it." I was pretty sure he had backed up far enough before he finished talking. He went a bit farther anyway.

I looked at Jason who mimed throwing a Frisbee and said, "Just like that."

I tried to do what Jason had done and the Frisbee hit the ground about three feet in front of me and rolled. Jason ran to pick it up and handed it back to me.

"That wasn't bad enough to prove my point?" I asked.

"Try again," he said. He showed me again. "Just pick your elbow up a bit and do it just like this."

I tried a few more times with the same results each time. Matt was laughing his head off. I didn't mind though because for some reason he seemed to be laughing at Jason. As though it was all his fault that I couldn't throw the stupid thing.

Jason tried to give the Frisbee back to me for what must have been the seventh or eighth attempt, but I'd had enough. I shook my head at him. "I give up. You guys just play."

Matt came back up to us. "One last time, Charlotte. I promise this is the last time. *Jason* will catch it." He pointed out into the field as though Jason was being banished from his sight.

I said, "Last time." I took the Frisbee.

Matt came around behind me and put his hand over mine. He showed me exactly how to move my arm. Then he took two steps back and said, "Do that."

I did. And I threw the Frisbee. It went maybe a quarter of the distance as when either of the guys threw it and didn't travel in anything resembling a straight line. But it was off the ground. The guys cheered for me, and not in a mocking way at all. Personally, I was much more impressed that Jason had caught my wayward toss.

After that, I told them I was quitting while I was ahead and they took my word for it. I watched for almost an hour. Frisbee is more fun to watch.

Chapter 14

I met Jason and Matt for several games that were more my style over the next two or three weeks. I was really starting to love the 4th floor lounge again. But there was something kind of gnawing at me. It was Abby. We had been sharing a room for more than two months and I still didn't know much more about her than I had when she moved in. We hardly spoke. We had our schedules posted in the room so we didn't even need to communicate our comings and goings. Sometimes we laughed at the same spot on a TV show, which was sort of like laughing together. That was about as far as our relationship had progressed. I was perfectly fine with that. Between Jason and Erin and Matt, I was feeling almost like a social butterfly. But I was beginning to wonder if Abby was fine with it.

She wasn't kicking me out for a boyfriend or filling our room with her friends. She didn't seem to be hanging out with anyone other than her grandparents. The next time I set up a meeting with the guys, I asked if they would mind if I invited Abby. They didn't mind. I asked Abby.

She said okay, but seemed a bit reluctant. I think it was nerves because she fit right in. She was the oldest of five and actually missed playing games with her siblings. Board games are good for non-talkers. You have your subject matter sitting on the table right in front of you. Within about two weeks, she told me that playing with us was more fun than at home. And not just because one of her brothers liked to cheat.

The four of us were meeting in the lounge nearly every day. Sometimes we didn't even have to make plans. We just all knew that that was our hangout. We didn't just play board games. Once we sat around eating ice cream together. We put another out-of-order sign on the TV. We went back to rearranging the furniture. We always put it back when we were done. Jason and I let Matt and Abby in on the secret of the creak in the couch.

Matt said, "Oh, I am so telling Mom that you did that."

Abby wanted to know why we didn't move to the 2nd floor lounge since the couch wasn't broken and it was right next to the guys' room anyway.

Jason thought that was funny. He said, "Ask Charlotte."

"Because this lounge is the best one."

"Why?" she asked.

"It just is."

Matt looked around the room. "Now I haven't actually been in the 3rd floor lounge, but I know the one on the 2nd looks exactly like this." He looked around again. "Exactly."

They all looked at me for an explanation. I couldn't give one. "It doesn't matter how they look. This one is still better. It just *feels* better."

Abby looked skeptical. "I bet you couldn't even tell the difference."

Jason got this look on his face like someone had just brought in the biggest Christmas present ever and said, "Oh! That would be an awesome experiment. You guys wait here." He ran from the room.

Matt looked at me. "I think you're in trouble."

I didn't know what was about to happen. I had a feeling though that Matt might be on to something. I might be in trouble. Jason came back a few minutes later with a black T-shirt. "Okay, I hope this works. It's the best I could come up with."

"For what?" I asked. I thought I knew the answer, but hoped I was wrong. I usually like to be right. I was willing to make an exception.

Jason grinned at me. "A blindfold." That's what I had guessed.

Matt and Abby cheered. They liked Jason's plan. I did not like the plan. I let them tie the blindfold on me anyway. It wasn't as bad as it could have been. The shirt smelled like Jason.

They spun me around the room first, which was completely unnecessary and they knew it. Then I was offered two hands. I could tell it was Jason and Abby. They led me to the elevator. We rode it up and down a few times. I heard the voice of someone I didn't know ask what we were doing. Then I heard Jason tell him it was an experiment for a Psych class. I knew when the extra person got out because my companions let out the laughs they had been holding in.

Finally, they led me out of the elevator.

"Okay," Jason told me, "we'll make it easy for you. You don't have to distinguish between the 2nd and 3rd floor lounges. Just say 4th or not 4th."

I wasn't looking forward to this. I knew I'd still insist the 4th floor was better no matter what happened. If I was wrong at all, they'd just have more ammo to tease me about it.

They led me into a room and began to squelch each other's giggles. I hoped no one else was in there watching us.

"Guess," Matt commanded me.

I'm not sure how I knew or even if I knew, but it didn't feel familiar so I said, "Not the 4th floor."

There were groans all around and a few mumbles of "lucky guess."

They took me back to the elevator. More ups and downs. Led me into another room.

"Guess again," Jason said.

I thought about it. "Still not the 4th floor."

More groans. More ups and downs in the elevator. Led me into another room. Way too much stifled laughter. Something was up.

"Now guess," Jason said.

It didn't feel right, like the walls were too close. "Um, guys… where am I? I don't think this is a lounge at all."

"Come on!" Matt and Jason let out similarly incredulous exclamations.

"How does she do that?" Abby wanted to know.

I tried to take off the blindfold. Jason stopped me. "Wait," he said. "Just one more time."

I sighed. He took my hand and pulled me along. We didn't get back in the elevator. Just walked around some sort of corner. As far as I could tell, we had just been standing in the stairwell next to the lounge. And now we were back in the lounge. The right lounge.

I smiled and said, "4th floor," before anyone asked me to guess.

Jason pulled off my blindfold and I enjoyed my moment of glory. And I enjoyed it again every time one of them brought it up. My friends now thought I had a weird talent. I guessed that was better than just being weird. Maybe.

****

Life was pretty good in and around the 4th floor lounge until there was another December and another problem. This time it was me.

We didn't do Christmas presents. I still didn't know if that was a guy thing, but I know that Matt thought it was. He said sometimes girls liked to give presents and that guys didn't and since we had a mixed group we should agree ahead of time that nobody would buy gifts. Abby protested. She said she liked buying presents even if she wasn't going to get any. Matt accused her of being a girl.

I was a little torn on the issue. I did like giving presents, but I didn't know what to get anyone. And I remembered how things had been sort of uneven the previous year. I thought it was good that we were talking about it ahead of time. Then Jason came up with a really good idea. He said we should go to the game store and pick out a new game. We could all chip in for it and it would be a present from everyone to everyone.

We all thought that was a good idea and not just because it was a good idea. Also because it gave us an excuse to head off campus together for a change. It sounded sort of almost like an adventure.

My car was closer than the one Jason and Matt shared so we all piled into it on a Saturday morning. I noticed that Abby had only spent one weekend with her grandparents since she started hanging out with us. I hoped they didn't mind too much. We went to a store that only sold games. Lots and lots of games. Possibly too many games because it took us about an hour and a half to agree on one. I texted Erin at one point to see if she had any ideas. She suggested Candyland. If I hadn't been getting so frustrated, I might have thought that was funny. Jason and Matt thought it was hilarious.

We eventually settled on something called *Ticket to Ride.* Matt had played it once before and I thought that was enough of a reason to get it because that meant I wouldn't have to be the one to explain it. Then we stopped for lunch and brought our new game home to try out. There was a huge study group in the 4th floor lounge. I don't know what they were thinking. Just because it was the weekend before exams didn't give them the right to take over our game space. We set up our game in the 3rd floor lounge. It was still fun. Mostly because my friends kept patting me on the back and asking if I needed a break from the "inferior lounge." They were being ridiculous. I loved it. It felt like we were really friends. Finally friends in a way I didn't have to analyze.

Then we had to pack up the game and pretend we were college students with exams coming up. We only got together with books for the next few days. It was nice, but it wasn't fun. Wednesday was the least fun. That was the day I discovered the problem.

It was Wednesday evening. Students were already trickling out for home. Abby was one of them. Her parents had arrived in town and she went to spend the night with them so they could all get an early start in the morning. I didn't envy the 11-hour drive two days in a row.

I had one more exam Thursday afternoon and had studied for it all I intended to. I knew both the guys had one more exam and that Matt was working pretty hard to prepare for his. So I texted Jason to see if he was free.

His reply: `I'm already in the lounge.`

I joined him. He was on the orange couch watching The Empire Strikes Back. He asked if I had seen it before. I said no because I hadn't. He tried to catch me up a bit during a commercial break. It was kind of obvious who the bad guys were though so I didn't need too much explanation. We watched for a while, not really saying much because we were both kind of worn out from exams and packing up some stuff to take home for the break. And because we didn't need to talk. It was comfortable silence.

I was thinking about that time I had dissolved into a pathetic mess on that same couch. Mostly because I was hoping Jason wasn't thinking about it. I was wondering if there was even the smallest teeny tiniest chance that he had forgotten about that. And I was also watching the movie. That's when something strange happened.

There's a scene where two of the characters kiss. I'm not talking a big make out session or anything. Just a few seconds and then it's over. But when they kissed I got the most inexplicable sensation that Jason was thinking about kissing *me*. Now, I can't read minds. Sometimes I'm not even all that good at reading what people are actually telling me. So I knew I imagined it. The problem was that I kept imagining it over and over again. All I could think about was how much I would like it if he kissed me. I couldn't even describe how much I would have liked it if he kissed me. I thought I would have been perfectly happy to let him check all my teeth. That's when I knew the problem was a big problem.

I remembered what had happened the last time romantic feelings crept into the 4th floor lounge. Several friendships, or what I thought were friendships, had been destroyed and I had been left something of a basketcase. I couldn't let that happen again. I couldn't let another group break up and I certainly couldn't be the cause of it. I'd be lost if I couldn't be friends with Jason. And that would probably mean I couldn't be friends with Matt. And what if they stopped hanging out with Abby without me and then she hated me for breaking up our group and I was left with a roommate who was openly hostile toward me? That would all be so bad.

Which was why I needed to be careful. And not like I had been careful with Adam because I had been really bad at being careful with Adam.

Chapter 15

Erin tried to cheer me up while I was home. She was very sympathetic about my problem with Jason. She had had a similar problem once and… no, not really. Erin hadn't had the falling for a friend problem. But she was still very sympathetic. And I described it so well she knew exactly what I was going through.

Things were going well with her guy. They were now officially a couple and he had taken her shoe shopping for Christmas. He told her to pick out a new favorite pair so she wouldn't obsess so much about the blue ones. I had a feeling I could now look forward to texts asking me to talk her out of the black shoes.

I went to church a lot when I was home because I was with my parents and they went to church a lot. There were four Sundays, plus Christmas and New Year's. I'm not going to admit how old I was when I realized we weren't going to church because it was New Year's.

I had lunch with my parents right before I planned to pack up and head back to school. That was when my mom said, "That wasn't so bad, was it?"

I looked down at the last few bites of my grilled cheese sandwich. My mom knew I loved grilled cheese so I didn't think that was what she was talking about.

"I mean going to church with us this morning. It wasn't torture?"

I shook my head. I actually kind of liked going to church because of the music and the pretty windows and the fact that I could wear a dress and not stick out like a sore thumb. I didn't admit any of that to my mom because I thought I might know what she was going to say next. I was right.

She said, "Then why don't you go when you're at school?"

I almost told her that it was because I didn't have anyone to sit with because that was the excuse I gave myself. But we would both know that it was an excuse. Even with my wonderful friends, I was still the kind of person who was happy with some alone time. My mom knew this about me as well as I did. So I simply told her that I didn't know why and I think I wasn't lying.

She said, "Just think about it."

So I did. That was another thing that was weird about me. I almost always did what my parents told me to do. I tried not to let anyone, including my parents, know this. But I couldn't help myself. Most of the time, they just seemed like reasonable people who happened to be pretty smart. I did not get the impression that this was true of other parents so it was possible that it was actually my parents who were weird.

I thought about going to church. By the time I got to my first Sunday of that second semester, I had decided that I wanted to go. It would be nice if I could say this was some sort of spiritual awakening. But I just missed the routine. Even though the building would be different than at home, the mass was always the same and I found routines comforting. And besides that, I had seen Jason twice and thought I might need some divine backup in my quest to be careful.

I was in for a bit of a shock. It turned out that I did have someone to sit with after all. Two someones. Jason and Matt were both there. I didn't sit with them though, they sat with me. They slipped into the pew next to me just as the organ started. And then I got another surprise. Matt could sing! I mean, I can carry a tune if it isn't too complicated and, you know, doesn't have too many notes in it. And Jason was doing all right. But Matt had something like talent. His voice was just… I know he's a guy and all, but it was just pretty. I didn't tell him that. I did sing a little quieter than usual myself though so I could listen. This church was even better than the one at home.

We walked out together and Jason said, "I didn't know you were Catholic."

I said, "I didn't know *you* were," which was true. One or maybe both guys had made occasional off-hand references to church, but I didn't know which church. And it hadn't come up that often. I never suggested that we get together Sunday mornings because I didn't want to broadcast the fact that I wasn't going to be at church. I told Jason my parents had given me a hard time about not going while I was home for Christmas. That was a little unfair to my parents. I thought they could handle it.

Jason said, "Yeah, I didn't go much last year, but Matt likes it and he'd totally tell on me if I didn't come with him."

I thought Matt probably liked it because he could show off his pipes. I started going to church with the guys every week after that and only partly because I wanted to be around when Matt showed off. I was a bit conflicted about the whole thing though. I hoped maybe God would help me get over my crush on Jason and then there he was sitting next to me. I didn't think that would help. Sometimes, during the homily, I'd glance over at Jason and wish I could reach out with the tip of my finger and trace his ear.

Yes, his *ear*. I was attracted to his ear. While I was in church. I'm pretty sure that solidifies my position as the weirdest person on the planet.

****

Jason had a birthday near the end of January. He had had one the previous January as well, but I hadn't known about that one. I wished I had known because it might have given me an excuse to contact him. But an excuse without courage might not have done me any good anyway.

His birthday was a Saturday. We decided that we should go out and do something special, or at least different, to mark the occasion. He was after all turning 21 and some people thought that was a milestone. I preferred even numbers myself.

We let him pick a movie and then we went to a restaurant for dinner. Matt and Abby sat on one side of the booth and I sat with Jason on the other. The guys had sat down first and I was really annoyed with them for not sitting on the same side because now it felt like some sort of double date. To me, that's what it felt like anyway. The three of them were all relaxed and happy and chatting like friends. And I was just thinking about how much I wished the booth was just a little bit bigger. Jason seemed so close that I couldn't think about anything except that he seemed so close. Except maybe the fact that he also smelled good.

I tried to focus on the good thing about him sitting next to me. That was that it was marginally better than him sitting right across from me. It would have been much more difficult to avoid looking at him then. I remembered how Adam had started to look at me differently and I wanted to make sure Jason couldn't see anything like that in my eyes.

It was January and it was dark when we left the restaurant so it was really cold on the way back to the car. I must have looked as cold as I felt because for a moment it looked as if Jason was going to put his arm around me to warm me up. He didn't. My imagination was going to have to learn how to behave itself.

We sang Happy Birthday to Jason in the car on the way home, which we all agreed was better than having the restaurant staff do it. Abby gave me a look during the song. I think she was noticing Matt's voice, too. He even made a simple song sound better. And not by adding in a bunch of extra notes or otherwise screwing with a perfectly good song. There was just something powerful in his voice that you couldn't ignore. I bet she thought it was pretty, too.

That funny double date vibe came back at the end of the evening when the guys insisted on walking us up to our room. I don't know why they did that.

The vibe changed as we got close because someone had written obscene messages on all the whiteboards in our hallway. There was one on our door, too. Matt got there first and wiped it away with his hand. "I can't believe someone did that," he said.

Abby shrugged. "Probably just someone's idea of a joke." Neither of the guys looked like they thought it was funny so she quickly added, "But obviously that person has no sense of humor."

"Has that happened before?" Jason asked.

Abby shook her head and I said, "No." There was actually a similar streak of messages when I was a freshman, but Jason looked more offended than I was so he didn't need to know that. I thought it best to talk about something else. "Today was fun," I said. "We should do it again for Abby's birthday." Abby's birthday wasn't until March. Just because I thought we should change the subject didn't mean I'd be any good at coming up with one.

Matt tried to run with it anyway. "Oh, no. You'd make us go to some sort of mushy, boring movie, wouldn't you?"

"It would depend on what was playing. But mushy and boring would not be out of the question."

"You'd pick a boring movie on purpose?"

"Well… Jason did."

"Hey, that wasn't boring." Jason still had to defend himself even though Abby was laughing. She was obviously teasing. It seemed that we could end the evening on a good note so Abby and I wished Jason a happy birthday one last time and we all said goodnight. We noticed that Jason and Matt cleared off several of the other girls' doors on their way back down the hall. Abby commented that that was very chivalrous of them. I quite agreed.

Chapter 16

Unfortunately, more vulgar messages popped up a few times over the next week or so. The writing itself didn't really bother me. It was easy enough to erase. But it seemed likely that it was the work of someone in the building and it was slightly unnerving to think of someone who thought that was funny living nearby.

I mostly tried to put it out of my mind. I never mentioned the notes to Jason or Matt. Abby did. She mentioned every one of them. She thought it was sweet that the guys seemed so protective of us.

"Another lovely message," she said as she floated into the lounge while the rest of us were setting up *Ticket to Ride*.

Matt shook his head. "If I figure out who's doing that…"

"I'll help you," Jason added.

They just sort of frowned for a moment and then went back to setting up the game. This was our third time with the game and I already noticed our little idiosyncrasies forming. Each player had dozens of tiny plastic train cars that he or she had to place on the board during the game. I liked to line mine up horizontally in front of me. Jason lined his up vertically. Abby arranged hers in squares, a big square with two smaller squares inside it. And Matt insisted on keeping all his cars in the bag until he needed them. I never felt weird when other people were being weird at the same time. It was a good game.

We were just about ready to start when I sensed a disturbance in the room. A bubbly-looking blond girl walked in and marched right up to our table. She hadn't said a word and already I knew she was a talker. She was holding a clipboard, which I didn't think was a good sign.

"Hey, guys. How are you?"

We all sort of nodded at her. Matt was eyeing the clipboard suspiciously.

"That looks like a fun game," she said.

We smiled politely, waiting for her to get to the point.

"Well, you know there's a Valentine's dance coming up, right?" She looked excited about this. Three of us gave her blank looks. Abby nodded. "I've been put in charge of doing all the decorations. I volunteered, actually. I think it's going to be really fun."

At this point, I thought I knew what was going on. I thought she was about to try to sell us tickets. But it was worse than that. None of us said anything so she just plowed right in.

"I still need to recruit a few more people to help me with the decorating and if I could count on all four of you… that would just be super. And everyone who helps gets a free ticket to the dance." She smiled expectantly.

That was her incentive? No wonder she hadn't recruited enough people.

"When exactly do you need help?" Abby asked. I thought this was really smart of her. The best way to get out of something like that was to look interested just until you could get enough details to craft a plausible excuse.

It was working. Blond girl thought she had someone on the hook. "The dance is next Saturday, which is actually the 12th. It starts at 8 o'clock. We're decorating the hall above the Student Union from 4 to 6 so you'd have lots of time to get ready. And, you know, with enough people helping we might even be done early."

Abby let out a breath and looked around at us. "What do you think, guys?" She was passing the baton. She had done the first part and now it was up to one of us to suddenly remember something else we had to do. We weren't fast enough because the next thing Abby said was, "I think we should help."

What!? Blond girl got her clipboard ready for our names while Jason and I looked at Abby like she was nuts. Matt also looked at her like she was nuts, but at the same time he said, "Well…" as though he was thinking about agreeing.

He looked at Jason. "Come on, man. We could all do it together."

Jason still didn't look thrilled, but he gave a tiny nod as though maybe, just maybe, he'd be game if everyone else was. I didn't know what was happening. I thought I knew these people.

Blond girl quickly began taking names, starting with Abby and then Matt and then Jason. She knew how to work this. Then she looked at me. They all looked at me. I hadn't said a thing and yet it was somehow assumed that I would go along with my friends. It was the first time I wasn't overjoyed to have these friends. I gave up my name.

But only because I had just latched on to a slight sliver of hope. Abby had said she thought we should *help*. Maybe she was just volunteering to help with the decorations out of her kind and generous nature and assuming her friends were kind and generous, too. We could go hang some streamers or something and then go do something that didn't involve too loud music and lots of people I didn't know who might try to talk to me over the too loud music and then ask me to repeat myself over and over because they couldn't hear me over the too loud music.

Blond girl was all smiles. "Okay, now we're going to give out the tickets while we're working so only people who actually show up can have them. And I don't know any of your situations here," she kind of waved her hand around the table, "but you only get one ticket each so you'll have to buy extra if you want to bring someone." She ducked out of the room in search of more victims.

Matt looked thoughtful. "Well, I guess we can go with just the four of us, right? We're nice and evenly matched so we won't look like losers who can't get dates. Unless… I mean, you can have my ticket if you wanted to bring a date."

His offer was directed at Abby. "Are you going to dance with me?" she asked.

"If I have to," he said.

"Then I don't need a date."

Abby didn't need a date, but she did, apparently, want to go to the dance. There went my last hope. Jason looked at me. "Do you mind being stuck with me?" he asked.

"Of course not," I said. It was a reflex. I never felt stuck with Jason. But I should have asked him if he really wanted to go. I should have said that we didn't have to go just because Matt and Abby were going. I should have said that because Jason always seemed to know when I was lying. In the brief moment I looked at him to answer there was a flash of pain in his eyes. How did he always know when I was lying? I was only thinking that a Valentine's dance could be a dangerous situation for someone who was trying so hard to be careful. And that I didn't want to go with anyone.

The game was a bit subdued at first. I believe that three of us were contemplating how we had been talked into attending a school function. And one of us, Abby, was gloating internally. I tried to look on the bright side. The dance was still over a week away. Perhaps the roof would cave in on the Student Union between now and then.

Matt was talking with Jason about one of his classes. Jason remembered taking it earlier. I was sort of half-listening. They said something about C-sharp, but it wasn't a music class. I was a bit lost.

"You're quiet today, Charlotte," Abby observed.

I said, "I'm always quiet." Had Abby suddenly forgotten that I was not a talker? Was that why we were going to a dance?

"No, you're different quiet. Are you that put out about this dance?"

Abby looked genuinely concerned. All of a sudden I felt the need to reassure her. If I wanted to have friends, then I needed to *be* a friend. This was the first favor she had asked in the months that I had known her. Okay, it was kind of a gargantuan favor, but still…

"No, I…the dance will be…" I couldn't bring myself to say fun. "It'll be all right."

"Oh, well…" Abby started rearranging the few train cars left in front of her. "I guess if you guys really don't want to… I mean…"

It was obvious that Abby wanted to go to this dance. I wasn't the only one who could tell.

"You can definitely count me in," Matt said. "Even if Charlotte and Jason decide to be spoil sports."

He was mostly looking at me. Jason was staying quiet. He was also fiddling with his train cars. I was the spoil sport. And now it would look like maybe my not wanting to go did have something to do with being stuck with Jason. I thought the best way to get us past this topic would be to come up with something else that could be bothering me. Oh, and I had thought of something already.

"Don't worry, Abby, I'm still going to the dance," if the roof doesn't come down, "I was actually thinking about something else. My accounting class always seems to leave me in a funk."

"Since when do you take accounting?" Matt asked.

Abby looked at me a little funny, like maybe she didn't believe me. "You're an English major."

I was going to have to do some full on venting to convince her. "I have to take some non-English classes in order to graduate. Something about making me well-rounded or something. I think they secretly just want me to appreciate the English classes. But anyway, in my accounting class… we have these groups."

I paused for a breath and Matt nodded. Jason said mockingly, "Poor Charlotte, a class with people in it."

I ignored him and continued. "Well, we constantly have these projects in class where we do something by ourselves and then split into our groups to compare answers. And it's really annoying because there are four girls in my group, including me, and two of them never do anything. They text each other back and forth when we're supposed to start the assignment and then gossip while me and the other girl figure out the right way to fill out the balance sheet or whatever we're working on. And honestly, I wouldn't care if they didn't help if they'd just shut up while we're working, but they never do. And the one girl I work with, well, I feel bad for saying this but she annoys me, too, even though she can't help it." I finished with a heavy sigh.

"What does she do?" Jason asked.

"It's mean I know, but… her name is Rhonda."

There was a bit of a pause because I didn't realize they were waiting for me to explain.

Then Matt said, "And how does Rhonda annoy you?"

"Oh, I know she can't help it. It's just her name."

"You're annoyed with someone because of her name?" Abby asked.

I nodded. I know I looked guilty.

Matt laughed and said, "I wonder if there's anyone who's annoyed at you for being named after a spider."

"I'm not named after a spider."

"Was it the pig?"

"No, the spider was named Charlotte. But that's not why I'm named Charlotte. My mom said she got the name from a novel she loved that had a beautiful heroine named Charlotte. People should look at me and think 'beautiful heroine,' not 'spider.'" I realized that was asking a lot so I sort of threw my hands up. "Okay, just think 'human character.'"

"You *are* a character, Charlotte." Abby was laughing at me now, too.

Then I noticed that Jason was singing quietly on my other side.

"Please, stop. I'm about to find you very annoying as well."

He started singing a bit louder, "Help me, Rhonda. Help, help me, Rhonda."

Matt and Abby were laughing. Abby said, "Is that why she annoys you?"

"Yes," I said. "Yes! Every day I leave class with that song in my head. It drives me nuts."

All three of them were singing. And none of them knew more than that one line of the song. They looked a lot happier teasing me than they did when we were talking about the dance.

Chapter 17

Now that we had what Abby called big plans, we needed to figure out what to wear. I let her look through my closet and she found the dress I wore to my brother's wedding the previous summer.

"Oh, this is perfect," she said. "I bet it looks really good on you."

"Yeah, it's okay." The dress was a sleeveless V-neck with crystal embellishments on the empire waist. My mom had picked it out for me and all my relatives said I looked nice. But I felt that the bright blue color – my mom called it electric blue – drew way too much attention to me. It was difficult to be a wallflower in a gregarious dress. I didn't have any intention of wearing it while I was at school. It was in my closet only because I had grabbed everything when I packed up my room at home.

Abby, however, seemed to think that was the only dress that would work for the dance. She seemed to know something about this because she had four cocktail dresses in her closet. She tried to get me to help her pick one. I pointed at the pink one because that was the one she looked most excited about. Then she went back to my closet and made a noise like she was disgusted with something.

"Charlotte, where are your shoes?"

I pointed to the floor of my closet.

"You don't have any shoes?"

I pointed to the floor of the closet again. There were clearly four pairs of shoes sitting there. "They're right there," I said.

Abby sighed and put her hands on her hips. "I mean to go with your dress."

"I can wear those black ones. That's what I wore last time."

Abby looked scandalized. "You need heels. I don't know how someone can like dresses as much as you do and not like to dress up."

"I don't like heels." This was true, but I didn't tell her why. She would probably assume that I thought they were uncomfortable or that I was too tall in heels. Those were not bad reasons. I didn't wear heels because I had never found a pair that didn't announce I was coming. I didn't wear shoes that clicked when I walked.

"Well, you can't wear any of those shoes." Abby said this as though she was telling me that the door was brown. "We're gonna have to go to the mall. We can go Saturday morning."

The mall!? It was bad enough she was dragging me to a dance. And now she wanted to take me to the mall? I was so not looking forward to Saturday.

****

Abby and I met the guys for dinner in the dining hall on Friday. I had my food first so I went to pick a table. While I was sitting there waiting for my friends, a completely random guy sat down next to me. He had long hair. Not as long as mine, but almost down to his shoulders.

He smiled broadly and said, "Hey, baby." Then he nodded at me. There was an expectant look on his face as though now it was my turn to say something as brilliant as hey. There was no way I was going to say hi so instead I said, "Someone is sitting there."

Long hair guy kept nodding, as though he was a bobble-head of himself. "I know," he said. "I'm sitting here."

"I mean someone else will be sitting there in a minute."

"Oh, so you're saying we don't have a lot of time together." Long hair guy gestured between us as though there was a we. "You better hurry up and give me your number then."

I shook my head. I hated to be rude even to someone who deserved it, but I could see Abby coming and knew Jason and Matt would be right behind her.

"Just go away… please," I said.

He sort of tipped his head as he stood up as though he was saying it was my loss and then he walked away.

Abby took his place. "Do you know that guy?"

"No."

"What did he want?"

"Nothing."

Abby took a bite of her sandwich. It looked like she was going to drop the subject. I was glad because now the guys had reached the table. But Matt looked at me as he put down his tray and said, "Was that guy hitting on you or something?"

Jason said, "What guy?"

"It was nothing," I said.

"It didn't look like nothing. It looked like he was hitting on you."

"Really?" Abby looked intrigued.

"Look. A guy sat down. Asked for my phone number. I told him to go away. End of story. Can we please eat now?"

"Sorry," Abby mumbled.

"No, I'm sorry. I shouldn't have snapped at you because someone else was a jerk." I was truly sorry. I knew that was going to be one of those conversations I relived in my head for the next several years and I would feel a twinge of embarrassment every single time. Most of the time I was so good at not talking. Why couldn't that have been one of those times? I thought it was only going to get worse by the look on Matt's face. He seemed to be trying to decide whether or not to say something that he wanted to say.

He must have decided to spit it out when he noticed me looking at him. He said, "Well, I get that you don't want to talk about it, but I'm a little confused." He paused for a moment to collect his thoughts. I was jealous of the filter. "It's just that… you said the guy only asked for your phone number and then you called him a jerk so I'm wondering… Did you leave something out of the conversation or is that all it takes?"

Now I was confused, too. "All what takes?"

"To be a jerk. I mean, I'm not trying to be one myself, but it takes a lot of guts to go up to a girl and ask for her number and I think maybe you're being a bit hard on him. Unless he said something you didn't tell us."

"What happened exactly?" Abby said.

"Well…" They were all looking at me expectantly and it seemed easier to tell them than to try to get onto a new subject. "All right, he sat down where Abby is and said hi."

"No wonder you called him a jerk," Matt said, grinning.

Abby told him to be quiet and let me finish.

"I told him someone was sitting there and he said, 'I know, I'm sitting here.'" Amusement. Maybe I was telling it wrong. I kept going anyway. "So I said, 'No, someone else is coming,' and he said that since we didn't have much time I should hurry up and give him my number. I, um, well, I asked him to *please* go away and he did."

It sounded kind of innocent when I told it. Matt obviously thought so. Maybe I shouldn't have insulted long hair guy. Maybe it wasn't his fault. I just couldn't explain that it wasn't what he said, but how he said it. Maybe it *would* take a lot of guts for Matt to ask for a phone number, but long hair guy didn't have that problem. He looked so comfortable talking to a complete stranger that I'd have been intimidated if he just asked what I was having for dinner. And that wasn't what he asked. He started a conversation with hormones and the potential for hurt feelings without looking like he had any feelings to hurt. That was completely unfair of him. I guessed it was also unfair for me to call him names because I was jealous of that skill.

Abby interrupted my muddled thoughts by asking why I didn't just give him my phone number.

"What!?"

"He was kind of cute and you're not dating anyone."

"Um…" Because I was scared. Terrified even. That's why I didn't give him my phone number. I couldn't admit that any more than I could admit that I wanted to be dating someone. Someone who was sitting across the table from me trying to look politely interested in the conversation. It was a good time to remember some words of wisdom from my mom. When faced with a question you don't want to answer, try deflecting with a question of your own. "Would you have given him your number?" I asked Abby.

She started to nod and then stopped and turned a bit red. "Actually, I did once. A guy came up to me near the start of school and I was so flattered that I gave him my number without thinking and then I spent the next two weeks in a panic over what to say if he called. And then he never did and I couldn't decide whether to be relieved or insulted."

Matt said, "Don't be insulted. He probably just chickened out." He looked like he knew what he was talking about. I decided to keep asking questions. It was working so far.

"Have you done that?" I looked at Matt. "Gotten a girl's phone number and then not called, I mean."

He laughed. "I told you it took a lot of guts to get the number in the first place. More guts than I have, apparently."

"Oh, I bet you could get some numbers," Abby said.

"I don't know. Charlotte would call me a jerk just for asking."

"I would not. In fact, you *have* my phone number." I flashed what I hoped was an ingratiating smile at him, wishing he'd let me off the hook for the careless insult.

"Okay, that's not the same thing at all and you know it."

It wasn't the same thing. I did know it. But I still hoped that would put an end to the conversation. But like with those rude messages that Abby kept telling the guys about, sometimes she just didn't know when to let something go. She was obviously coming up with another question and she was looking at me. I didn't think that could be good. I was right.

"Well, when would you give a guy your phone number?" she asked me.

"Um… what do you mean?" I didn't really want the answer to that. It was the first question that popped into my head.

"I guess I don't mean a phone number so much as a date. That's kind of the point of giving out the phone number."

"Is there a question in there?" I was so failing at deflecting.

"I just mean that I know you get hit on a lot, but you don't seem to ever go out with anyone. What are you waiting for?"

"I'm not waiting. I mean, I have been on a few dates. I just…" I picked up my drink and took a long sip. I needed to figure out how to answer this without embarrassing myself or Jason. He was being so quiet. I didn't think he liked this topic any more than I did. If the four of us were really good friends though, we should be able to talk about things that might be uncomfortable, right? After all, I would not have given my number to long hair guy even if I wasn't secretly nuts about Jason. I needed to focus on that. "I guess I'm just waiting for someone to give me a serious offer. I need a better reason to go out with someone than 'Hey, baby.'"

Jason wrinkled his brow. "Did that guy who was here before call you baby?"

I nodded.

"Oh, you said he said hi."

"I was paraphrasing."

"'Hey, baby' is not the same thing as 'hi,'" Jason said.

"Totally not," Matt agreed. "I take everything back. You were right to call him a jerk."

Chapter 18

I woke up Saturday morning and immediately remembered all the really fun stuff that was planned for me. I thought about staying in bed all day. Abby was already up. I could hear her moving around the room and quietly talking to herself. She sounded happy. I went ahead and pushed the covers back.

"Oh, I'm glad you're up," she said. "Go look at the door. Someone left a message for you."

It had been about a week since we had received one of those vulgar messages. I didn't know if the culprit had been caught or just got tired of his own lameness, but I knew Abby wouldn't send me into the hall to look at one of those messages anyway. I opened the door and saw that someone had written "Charlotte, I love you" on the whiteboard.

I erased the board and then closed the door. I started looking for something to wear.

"That's it!?" Abby said. "You don't even look like you want to know who wrote it."

I shrugged at her. "It doesn't mean anything. It's like that guy last night or those guys who used to write on our board all the time." That had stopped as soon as I rejected Keith. I did wonder if maybe one of those guys would think this new message was funny.

Abby looked at me as though I was a small child. "There's a big difference in writing '*We* love you' and writing '*I* love you.' I think someone has a real crush on you."

"Well, even if you were right, which you're not, there's nothing I can do about it."

"You have to figure out who it is. It has to be someone who knows your name and where you live."

"Yeah, that narrows it down to any guy in any of my classes who happens to have access to a student directory."

Abby looked a bit less excited. "Hmm... that's probably still a lot of guys. Is there anyone you talk to during class?"

I gave Abby a look. She seemed to realize that was a stupid question. Sometimes when we're together we forget that we're not talkers. She opened her mouth for a second as though she had another idea, but then she didn't say anything. Instead, she asked when I'd be ready to go to the mall. I wished I had a look to let her know exactly what I thought of that.

Three hours later, I had a new pair of shoes. And no, it did not take three hours to pick out shoes. When I had that conversation with Abby, I hadn't even had breakfast yet. And we had to get my car and drive to the mall and all that. I guess I'm a little sensitive about how long the shopping actually took because Abby was getting pretty frustrated with me by the end of it. She didn't seem to understand exactly what I was looking for. That might be partly my fault. I didn't tell her.

I liked the shoes I ended up with though. They were very simple and very quiet and Abby approved as well. We were walking back through the mall with my new purchase in hand when Abby said, "I think we're being followed again."

I looked in the direction she had tilted her head and saw three guys pacing us on the opposite side of the hall. One of them waved at me.

"Just ignore them," I muttered.

"You know, I had a friend in high school who always wanted me to come to the mall with her. She came specifically to try to meet guys and… well, I'm just amazed at how different it is with you. We're getting a lot more attention without even trying."

"Yeah, I'm sorry about that. I don't understand it either."

Abby laughed at me. Laughed so hard she stopped walking. I turned to look at her. "What's to understand?" she said. "Guys look at you because you're hot."

I didn't think Abby knew what she was talking about. I mean, I wasn't blind. I knew I had proportions similar to women in magazines. But I also knew it took more than that to be hot. I've seen those movies where the girl isn't pretty until she takes her glasses off. I didn't wear glasses, but that wasn't exactly the point. Abby seemed to think that didn't matter.

"You sure put me to shame. I bet everyone here thinks I'm your baby sister."

"You're not that much younger than me."

"I'm talking about how young I look. People think I'm not even done growing yet."

"Come on, you're not *that* short."

"Okay, well, you put almost that short with this baby face… the whole package says 14."

I looked at Abby. Really looked at her. She didn't look 14 and I thought I should tell her that, but I didn't know how to explain it. That didn't stop me from trying. "You don't look that young. Really, there's just something… It's like your eyes have too much attitude for a 14-year-old."

Abby thought that was funny. She thanked me anyway.

****

We planned to meet Jason and Matt at the front doors just before 4 o'clock so we could all walk over to the Student Union together. They were waiting for us when we came down the stairs. I noticed that Jason was staring at the floor and he seemed nervous. It was probably dread. I was glad he was looking at the floor though because I had been avoiding his eyes. Since he wasn't looking at me I was free to look at him. His hair was sticking up more than usual as though he'd been running his hands through it. His jacket was unzipped and I could see that he was wearing that blue shirt that made his eyes look even bluer. I'd have to look away before I could enjoy that. I was afraid that if he saw my eyes he'd know exactly what I was thinking and that would be the start of everything falling apart. What if he wasn't any better at being careful with me than I had been with Adam?

I wasn't quite fast enough. His eyes jumped up to mine expectantly, like he was asking a question. I assumed the question was, "Are you ready to get this over with?" so that's what I said as I turned quickly to look at Matt. He was safer.

Matt nodded and grabbed the door.

"Come on," Abby said. "Let's have a positive attitude here. You guys might even have fun."

I doubted that. I reminded myself to try to be a good sport as I walked through the door that Matt held open. Jason lagged behind as we walked over and I slowed down to walk with him. Neither of us said anything. It was great that we could just walk together and be comfortable. Well, as comfortable as two people can be walking when it's 40 degrees.

"Charlotte?"

I realized I had taken a few steps without Jason. He was standing on a corner. Matt and Abby were ahead of him, cutting the diagonal through the grass. He gestured after them and said, "We're going this way."

"Oh, I… the sidewalk is over here."

"But this way is faster."

"Yeah, maybe, but…"

"There's no maybe. It's a triangle. The diagonal is shorter and therefore faster. You can see the path worn in the grass because everyone else knows this way is faster."

I didn't know what to say. I thought Jason had gotten used to me by now. I couldn't explain why I needed to walk on the sidewalk. But… for crying out loud, it has the word walk in its name. I'm supposed to ignore that?

I think I was looking at Jason kind of helplessly when a huge grin stretched across his face. He said, "You like the sidewalk like you like the 4th floor lounge, don't you?"

I smiled, too. He did get me.

Jason glanced over at Matt and Abby, who didn't seem to realize we had stopped. "Okay," he said. "But we have to run." He kept grinning as he grabbed my hand and started pulling me along. I was so surprised I couldn't do anything but run after him. It took me a minute to realize that it was a race.

We had rounded the corner by the time Matt realized it as well. And that he was losing. "Oh, no, you don't!" he yelled as he started running, too.

In the end it was really close. Jason would have been way ahead if I hadn't been slowing him down, but we just reached the door before Matt. We were all laughing when Abby jogged up a bit later.

"For people who aren't thrilled about this, you sure are in a hurry to get here," she said.

Matt told her that she was the one who said we should have a positive attitude.

As soon as we went inside, we met the blond girl who had signed us up. She remembered all of our names. I mean, I know she had them written down and everything, but she remembered who was who. Then she put us to work.

Abby and I were in charge of blowing up balloons. They had a tank for that so it didn't make me dizzy. My fingers got the hang of the tying after a few times. I was glad the balloons were a big project. I was happy to stay in one place during the decorating.

Blond girl was impressive at getting everyone organized. It's good that there are people who are good at that sort of thing because I knew I'd never be one of them. She put everyone else to work moving tables and chairs around first. There were four or five people I didn't know who were helping, all of them girls. I noticed that one of those girls seemed to be looking at Jason a lot. But she stopped when she realized that he was looking at me just as much.

Jason was looking at me because he was messing around with the decorations and wanted to see if he could make me laugh. Blond girl had given him giant letters to write Happy Valentine's Day on the wall and he spelled it wrong on purpose just to see how long it took her to point it out. Matt was busy sticking shiny paperboard hearts around the room. Jason grabbed one when he wasn't looking and stuck it to his back. He winked at me when he did it and that made me let go of the balloon I was attempting to tie. It went flying around the room and I think Jason thought I did it on purpose. Blond girl did, too, but she didn't look as amused.

Abby and I had been putting all our balloons into a big net. The last step in the decorating was to suspend the net just below the ceiling. Now I was there. I didn't help, but I watched. And I still don't know how it was accomplished. It did look nice though.

Then blond girl congratulated us on being done early. It was 10 minutes before 6 o'clock, which I suppose was technically early. She handed out tickets and we went back to change and get dinner. Abby told the guys we didn't have time to eat with them because we had to get ready. We took our food back to our room. Afterword, I washed my face and put on my blue dress and new shoes. Then I sat on the edge of my bed watching Abby.

I didn't know she had a curling iron, but it turned out that she had at least two of them. I think she spent almost an hour on her hair. She spent time adding more make-up as well. I started to worry. How out of place was I going to look when all the other girls had special hair? I had so much hair that doing anything with it seemed overwhelming. Abby finished with herself and then I don't know if she sensed how uncomfortable I was or if she just didn't want to be seen with someone who was so obviously clueless, but she insisted that I borrow one of her necklaces and put a sparkly clip in the side of my hair. Then she muttered something to herself about hating how easy it was for me. I felt bad for a second even though it was a compliment.

Just before putting on my coat, I checked my reflection in the mirror. I thought I looked like I had taken my glasses off. I still didn't wear glasses. It was like figurative glasses. Abby had made me look good. And she'd done a pretty fabulous job on herself as well. I still didn't want to go to the dance. I was, however, beginning to understand why Abby liked the dressing up part of it.

We bundled up and went down to meet Jason and Matt. They were both wearing black suits and they looked more alike than usual. Except that Jason still looked better. For a minute I forgot that I was trying not to look at him.

The guys were not wearing coats over their suits and Abby and I had our legs exposed so we walked pretty quickly. We talked about the decorations a bit and Matt said that Abby and I sure did fill a lot of balloons. I said that I filled 82 and looked at Abby because we could add our numbers and know exactly how many were in the net. She looked back at me as though maybe it was weird that I knew how many balloons I had filled.

I sighed and hung my head. I could hear all three of them trying unsuccessfully to stifle some laughter.

I said, "You guys are laughing with me now, right? With me?" And that made Jason stop trying to stifle anything. I hoped that was because he remembered saying that to me once.

We could see other people, mostly couples, heading the same way we were. When we reached that corner where the sidewalk turns, Jason was the first one to follow it. Matt asked him why he was going the long way.

Jason said, "The sidewalk is just better. Charlotte and I will meet you there."

Matt and Abby didn't stop to ask any more questions. I think they were cold. They were waiting for us just inside the door. Abby and I hung up our coats and Matt nudged his brother and said people were going to think they had done pretty well for themselves. I think I knew what he meant because it felt like a compliment. I especially liked the way it felt when Jason agreed with him.

Chapter 19

When we went into the hall we had decorated earlier, I finally figured out why Abby had wanted to go to the dance in the first place. Apparently, she really liked to dance. I envied the way she didn't seem to care whether or not she looked stupid. Mostly because I think that was what made her *not* look stupid. I don't know about the guys. I figured that standing there not dancing would attract more attention than dancing a little and that as long as I moved around less than Abby, people would be looking at her instead of me. I don't know if that was a good strategy. I kept telling myself it was working though because that was the only way I could relax at all.

The DJ switched to a slower song. Jason and I were off the hook for a bit. Abby only needed Matt for slow songs. I looked at Jason and pointed to some chairs nearby. He nodded and we went to sit down. We didn't try to talk because the music was as loud as I thought it would be. We just watched people for a while.

A second slow song started and a guy immediately appeared in the chair on my left. I had no idea where he came from. He asked if I wanted to dance.

I said, "No, thanks."

He said, "What?"

I said, "No, thanks," as loudly as I could. He left. I think that was the most polite way I could have refused him, but nothing feels polite when you're yelling it at someone. Soon the music sped up and Matt and Abby were back to drag us out of our chairs.

Abby was working hard to get the rest of us into her groove. She tried to get us to copy some of her moves. I did and I admit I had a modicum of fun. But when the music slowed down, I made a beeline for that same chair. Jason was right behind me. We had barely sat down when I noticed another guy walking towards us. All of a sudden I remembered how that girl had stopped looking at Jason when she thought we were together. I plopped my hand palm up in Jason's lap and commanded him to hold it. He did, but looked a little confused. I swung my eyes toward the guy who was now turning around. Jason nodded his understanding.

Matt and Abby popped up next to us a minute or two later, both of them smirking broadly. Matt asked if there was something going on and I realized I was still holding Jason's hand. Jason shrugged at his brother and said, "She's using me as guy repellant."

Matt laughed and gave me a thumb's up. I think he said, "Good thinking," but it was kind of hard to tell over the music. Abby quickly pulled him backwards again. I wondered if she thought she'd never get the three of us to another dance and was trying to make the most of it. And I wondered at how I could have forgotten I was holding Jason's hand. A month ago I had been freaking out at the slightest touch. Don't get me wrong, sitting so close still made my hair feel lighter. I was getting used to it though. I was no longer surprised that I felt warm when he smiled at me.

It was different now. I didn't just have a crush on him. I think I was finding out what it was like to be in love with someone.

Was that good or bad?

I was pretty sure that didn't help my situation, but decided that it didn't matter as long as I was the only one who knew. For now it just meant that I wanted Jason to be happy. I looked at him. He didn't look happy. In fact, he seemed to be approaching miserable. I leaned over and said, "Are we having fun yet?"

He smiled.

I told him we could leave whenever he was ready to go.

His mouth said, "If you're sure," and his eyes said, "Thank you for getting me out of here."

But when we stood up and I thought we'd head straight for the exit, Jason pulled me towards the dancing couples. He said, "Maybe just one dance? Since we're here and all."

Like I was going to refuse. I might have suggested it myself if I hadn't been sure Jason would reject the idea. I guess I was wrong about that. I still had to warn him though. "Okay, but I dance like I throw a Frisbee."

He laughed and said, "That's all right. I dance like you throw a Frisbee, too."

We were both right. We spent most of the song trying to figure out what other people were doing. It was kind of pathetic. I loved it. We stood close and laughed at ourselves. And Jason looked much happier than he had sitting by the wall. When the music sped up he asked if I still wanted to leave.

I did. I excused myself to find a restroom first. I came out and saw Abby right away. She was hard to miss. Matt was right beside her still trying to figure out what to do. Jason wasn't with them. I noticed a punch table and decided I was thirsty enough to get a drink while I looked for him. I picked up a cup without acknowledging the girl filling them. Still didn't see Jason anywhere.

I jumped headfirst into a nice little daydream. Mostly I was remembering that dance. Remembering the last few seconds when I had put my head against his shoulder. Those had been a great few seconds even though it reminded me of the other time my head touched his shoulder. A weird thought came into my head. Was it possible that I had been in love with him since then and just too stupid to realize it? I was a great student. But socially… I might just have been that stupid.

Suddenly I heard a whisper of "Earth to Charlotte," in my ear that made me flinch so badly I splashed the nice red punch onto Jason's nice white sleeve. I apologized profusely and he said he shouldn't have snuck up on someone with a weapon. Then he said that at least it gave us an excuse to leave if Abby caught us slipping out early. That was a good point, but it didn't make me feel any better about being a klutz.

Jason walked outside with his suit coat just over his shoulders, presumably not to get punch on the inside of the sleeve. I thought he must be even more freezing than I was so I hurried along the path in the grass. He asked what I was doing and when I said, "Aren't you cold?" he followed me without saying anything about how it was weird that I wasn't being weird.

I followed Jason to his room where he went in just long enough to swap his jacket for a bottle of laundry soap. There was someone else in the laundry room. A guy with big ears who was sitting there with his arms crossed watching clothes spin in one of the dryers. He kind of jerked his head at us when we came in which I think was sort of like a greeting.

Jason set the bottle down on a closed washing machine and looked at it uncertainly. "Is that what we need?" he asked.

"I don't know. Do you have anything else?"

He shook his head. "I guess that will have to work," he said as he loosened his tie and pulled it over his head. I stepped forward and began to undo the buttons on his shirt because… well, I don't really know what I was thinking other than it was my fault he had punch on his shirt and I should probably do something to help.

I think I was being a little too helpful though because big ear guy said, "Uh, do you guys need me to leave?"

That's when I noticed several things all at once… how what I was doing might look, how I had made Jason turn red, and how it might have been better when I was afraid to touch him. I took a huge step backward and said, "You can probably do that yourself."

I thought I shouldn't look at anyone for a minute because I could feel myself blushing as well. I turned the back of the laundry soap towards me so I could see if it had any instructions on how to clean up after being an idiot. It didn't have advice specific to punch stains either.

Once Jason was down to his white T-shirt, which looked awesome on him but I think I managed to pretend I didn't notice, I thought it might be safe to help again. I took off my jacket so I wouldn't get my sleeves wet. Unfortunately, that got big ear guy's attention. He unfolded his arms and was no longer watching us out of the corner of his eye. Now he was blatantly staring at me. And not at my face. I can't believe it was my mother who thought electric blue was a good idea.

I tried really hard to ignore big ear guy's palpable ogling. Jason was examining the sleeve. "Do you think we should rub some soap in or just let it soak or what?" he asked.

"I don't know. I'm going to suggest we try rubbing it first because we might know if it's working faster."

Jason sort of half shrugged and half nodded. I could see big ear guy over his shoulder still looking at me as though he was trying to see right through my dress. I didn't want to think about the fact that he might be doing exactly that so I snatched the shirt from Jason and turned to the sink. I poured a few drops of soap on the sleeve and rubbed it together the way I think I once saw someone do in a commercial.

The dryer shut off and I could tell big ear guy was getting his clothes. I couldn't wait for him to leave because he was giving me the creeps.

I was still working furiously with the shirt when the door closed behind big ear guy. I tried to relax but now that I was paying attention to what I was doing I could see that, while it did look better, there were still pink spots.

Jason put one of his hands on mine to slow them down and he said, "Maybe we should just let that soak for a minute."

If I hadn't been exhausted from doing things I didn't want to do all day or completely unnerved by big ear guy leering at me or annoyed with myself for spilling the punch, then I might have noticed that Jason sounded kind of funny when he said it or that the way his fingers slid around on mine didn't have anything to do with the soap or that he might have wanted me to put the shirt down because he was trying to get my attention. But I didn't notice any of that because I *was* exhausted and unnerved and annoyed that I had messed up an evening that wasn't all that great to begin with.

So I dropped the shirt into the sink and said, "Maybe I should call my mom and see if she knows what to do."

Jason sighed and stepped back. I thought he must be giving up on the stain. He didn't say anything right away, but then he said not to bother anyone, that he'd just let it soak for a bit and if it didn't come out that he could always buy a new shirt. I told him if it came to that he'd have to let me pay for it and he said again that it was his fault for startling me.

He looked so tired that I didn't want to argue with him right then. And I yawned and tried to cover up the fact that I was yawning. It wasn't that late. The day of activities was just taking its toll on me. Jason took pity on me and sent me back to my room to get ready for bed. He promised to finish in the laundry room quickly so I left him there.

I perked up a bit after my shower and sent Erin a text just before I climbed under my covers. It said: `The dance was just as boring as I expected except for the part when I tried to take Jason's clothes off.`

That sounded more exciting than what actually happened. I thought Erin would enjoy it.

Chapter 20

Abby must have stayed out pretty late because I wasn't pretending to sleep when she came in and she wasn't pretending when I got dressed for church in the morning. I quietly opened the door to get some breakfast and noticed a note on the board. I knew it was for me even though it didn't have my name on it because I recognized the handwriting from the previous day. It said, "Why don't you know it was me?"

Normally, I'm an eraser only sort of person, or at least a tissue, but I used my fingers to smear that message away because it made me angry. I felt like someone was calling me an idiot for not realizing that some guy had been staring at the back of my head during class. Guys stared at me all the time and now one of them wanted me to think I hurt his feelings by not turning around at the right time. I didn't want to feel bad about something that wasn't my fault.

****

Jason wasn't at church that morning. Matt said he wasn't feeling well. Then he asked me if I had talked to Abby. I explained about the not pretending to sleep. I explained the part that would make sense to him anyway. He seemed kind of happy about something during the mass. I didn't talk to him much afterwards so I didn't find out what it was. I had to work later in the afternoon and I was a little behind on homework so I didn't really talk to anybody most of the day.

When I got back to my room that night, Matt and Abby were standing in front of the door. I suspected that there might be something going on between them because they were kissing.

They stopped and smiled when they saw me coming. They had the decency to look embarrassed. I didn't say anything as I put my key in the lock and let myself into the room.

I had assumed that any sort of romantic feelings would disintegrate our little group. But I had never considered what would happen if those feelings went both ways so I couldn't figure out whether or not I should freak out about this new development. I was still trying to figure it out when Abby came in a few minutes later smiling from ear to ear and said, "Isn't it great!?"

I nodded, but I didn't know. I was working really hard to decide whether or not it was great. I still thought maybe I should freak out. I kind of thought Abby should freak out, too. She just looked really happy though. I realized that freaking out would be the selfish thing to do. I couldn't think about how this might affect me. I had to think about my two friends who were now happy together. I told her that I was happy for her. I was sure that would be true as soon as I finished freaking out.

****

The four of us had recently worked out a standing appointment on Tuesday nights to play Tichu, which Matt had slightly less recently decided was his favorite game. Tichu needed four players. I hoped that even though Matt and Abby were now a couple they would still need me and Jason for Tuesday nights. But I worried about that first one. Would it be tense now? Would their goo-goo eyes make me and Jason want to leave the room? Would they cancel altogether to be alone? Was this the end of me having friends at school?

In my panicked state, I started saying hi to a quiet girl in one of my classes just in case I needed to work on a new friendship. I progressed the relationship to the point that I thought of her as "Beth from Canadian Fiction" instead of "that girl who sits next to me in Canadian Fiction" so that I could worry less about becoming lonely.

Erin tried to talk me down. She said it wasn't like the last time. Jason had likely backed off then so as not to be a third wheel and surely he and I could hang out even if Matt and Abby wanted to do their own thing. And I would still have Abby as a roommate I could talk to. I thought Erin might have been right about everything. I just would have felt better if I had seen it coming.

That first Tuesday game was pretty normal. We played guys versus girls, which was fairly standard for team games. There were the same taunts and the same reminders about that rule no one could remember. The only tense moment actually had nothing to do with the budding relationship. It was my fault. I overreacted again. Abby had seen that second message on our door and she didn't know how much it bothered me. She insisted on teasing me about it. She kept asking why I didn't know things. Matt caught on to the joke eventually and asked what was going on.

"Oh, Charlotte didn't tell you guys that she has a secret admirer?"

Matt kind of snorted. "Charlotte has a lot of admirers and they're not all that secret."

"No, this is different. Love notes and everything."

"Really?" Matt looked at me with his left eyebrow slightly raised. Actually, I think it was my left and his right.

"It's not different," I said.

Abby shook her head. Having a new boyfriend clearly made her an expert on my nonexistent love life. "Charlotte, I think it's different. I think you should find out…"

"No," I cut her off. "I'm not interested."

"But you don't even know who…"

"I said I wasn't interested and I don't want to talk about it." I think I sort of yelled a bit. I'm not a talker and I'm really not a yeller. I tried to focus on my cards while Abby clamped her mouth closed. Neither of the guys said anything. The game was rather subdued for a few minutes. But then Matt got a hand with two bombs and the game got interesting enough for everyone to forget what I didn't want to talk about. By the end of the evening, I only noticed two differences. The first was that Matt took Abby's hand as they left the room and the second was that Jason looked like he was trying not to look sad. I assumed he was concerned about the new dynamic as well.

He still laughed when Matt told a funny story about one of his classes and he still barked when he played the dog card. I thought it was possible I only imagined that he seemed sad. Like when I imagined that Erin's parents didn't like me or when I imagined that my mom liked scarves. All through junior high I thought my mom liked scarves. Then one day Andy told me that I should stop being stupid because when was the last time I saw mom wear a scarf. At first, I imagined that Andy was just being my annoying brother. But then I realized that mom never did wear scarves and I would need to think of something else to get her for Christmas that year.

I thought I might be imagining that there was something bothering Jason just because I wanted an excuse to try to see him more often. But if I did, that was a really bad excuse because what was I going to do? Talk him into feeling better? That wasn't exactly in my skill set.

The new normal set in over the next few weeks and it wasn't so bad. Abby started going to church with us. We went out for lunch afterwards. Matt didn't seem likely to get tired of Tichu any time soon and even though he and Abby sometimes wanted to be alone, they never kicked me out of my room to accomplish that.

Tuesday and Sunday should have been enough for me. Especially considering the social ease of standing appointments. I still felt like something was missing though. It was Jason's fault. He was always being so nice to me. I realized that I was only going to be okay being his friend as long as he wasn't dating anyone. I decided that I should try to see him more often, just the two of us, and outside the 4th floor lounge. I was such a conniving rat. My plan was for other girls to see us together so they'd assume we were dating and then they'd leave him alone. Isn't that terrible? I was going to have to go to confession if it worked.

I texted him on a Wednesday and asked if he wanted to meet me for dinner. Abby told me that she and Matt already had plans. That seemed like a good excuse to only ask Jason.

He replied: `Okay.  I was going to eat anyway.`

I think he was being casual and not dismissive. I was just happy he agreed.

I was standing by the door to the dining hall avoiding eye contact with others when I almost avoided Jason by mistake. Jason was a plain T-shirt and jeans guy. I got to see him in a suit for that Valentine's dance of course and I think he might have worn shorts occasionally when it was warmer. The suit made sense for the occasion and shorts made sense for the weather. But I didn't see the sense in the shirt he had on that day. It was a long sleeved polo with red, green and white stripes. The collar was red, too. The whole thing was messing with my head. It was clearly the shirt of an extrovert and I hadn't invited that shirt to dinner.

I didn't say anything about the shirt. I just asked what sort of food he was in the mood for. Jason, not the shirt. I didn't care what it wanted to eat. We went in and looked at our choices. It turned out that Jason was in the mood for mac and cheese. He just didn't know that until he saw it. I didn't know I wanted mac and cheese until I saw Jason scoop the gooey goodness onto his plate. Sometimes at school the mac and cheese looked dry, like it had been sitting out longer than necessary. And sometimes it looked runny, like it had already gotten dry and then been doused with milk. It was fresh and cheesy that day so I didn't have to worry about Jason thinking it was weird that I liked it anyway. He already knew about a few quirks and seemed to like me anyway. That didn't mean I was ready to show my full array of oddities. I was, after all, trying to *increase* the amount of time he was willing to spend with me while proving that we didn't need other people to be friends.

Jason complimented my dress as we sat down to eat. He just said he liked it. It was a navy blue sweater dress and one of the few I had that were warm enough to wear in March. I think I said something about how the dress was warm enough to wear in March. Then I started obsessing about how it would be nice to compliment Jason as well and how that was going to be impossible to do. I couldn't say that the way he had just smiled at me was now the highlight of my day because I was pretty sure that was not the kind of thing you say to someone who was just a friend and I couldn't tell him that I liked his funny shirt because I knew he wouldn't believe me. The smile and the shirt were the only ideas that popped into my head and I didn't want to invite a sappy expression by sitting there thinking up other things I liked about Jason. He was going to have to do without a compliment for the moment. I focused on my dinner.

He said, "We got to turn in that big project today so I'm kind of celebrating."

I nodded because I had just taken a bite. Jason had been late for Tichu the previous day because of a meeting that went long. It was for a group project. He seemed to feel about group projects the way I felt about splinters, which I liked only marginally more than I liked group projects.

"Congratulations," I said after I swallowed. "I guess that means you got it done this afternoon?"

Jason rolled his eyes. "Barely. I really thought Jack and Conner were going to come to blows before the end."

"Conner was the idiot, right?"

"Yeah."

That was Jason's word. Idiot. He had been working on the project for a few weeks and explained that one of the guys, Conner apparently, thought that he should be in charge and everyone else in the group thought he was an idiot for not realizing that he was the least qualified to be in charge. Because he was an idiot. The Tuesday night meeting had been arranged behind Conner's back. "Did he figure out what you guys were up to?"

Jason shook his head. Then he smiled. "You give him too much credit."

"Well, I've never met him. I always wonder if you're exaggerating."

"Me exaggerate?" He tried to look innocent. I thought he might have pulled it off if he had been wearing a normal shirt.

"Not even when you said he called an apostrophe a high comma?"

Jason almost choked on his drink. When he recovered, he said, "He honestly said that. He tried to play it off as though he was being stupid on purpose and I admit he might have been. But a joke like that only works if you're not already known as the world's biggest idiot."

"I don't think that joke would work for anyone."

"Really? You wouldn't laugh if I renamed punctuation?"

I tried to be coy and said, "Maybe." I would probably laugh. That wouldn't mean it would be funny. I wondered if Jason was trying to come up with a silly name for a question mark. Then my phone buzzed. I ignored it, but Jason noticed it, too.

"I don't mind if you check that. It's probably Erin, right?"

I shrugged and pulled the phone out of my purse, which was sitting on the chair next to me. I usually shared Erin's random texts with Jason. She didn't mind and he seemed to enjoy them almost as much as I did. It was Erin. I would not be sharing her message. It said: `Have you scared away all the other girls yet?`

Erin knew I'd still be with Jason when I got that message. Sometimes she wasn't as funny as she thought she was. I stuffed the phone back into the bag and zipped it. I didn't usually bother with the zipper.

"Not Erin?" Jason said.

"Umm… It was… I don't know."

Jason was giving me a strange look. I thought it might have something to do with the fact that I acted like I didn't know how to answer a simple question. He never asked me what she said. I would just volunteer if it was something interesting. I didn't have to be evasive and now he knew something was up because I gave a nonsense answer. Great. I tried again. "That was Erin. She was just trying to embarrass me." My checks were a bit warm so she had succeeded. It was possible that I embarrassed myself. I'd rather blame Erin.

Jason respectfully looked at his plate while I recovered. But then he said, "I hope I get to meet Erin someday. She must have a lot of good dirt on you."

"If you ever meet her, you are not allowed to ask her for embarrassing stories."

He looked up with skepticism all over his face. "I'm not *allowed*."

"Absolutely not. You should remember that I know your brother."

Jason's expression changed. He appeared to be thinking fast. "Well... I don't... yeah, I've thought about it and I'm pretty sure that I've never done anything embarrassing so... you can ask Matt anything you want."

"Maybe I will."

I had no idea if I would do that. I liked the idea of hearing stories about Jason, but no one liked to feel embarrassed. I didn't want to do that to him. But I might if he provoked me. I reached for my drink. We were going to be done eating soon and I wondered if there was any way I could extend our time together. I asked if he had anything planned for after dinner.

"That should be obvious," he laughed and glanced down at his shirt at the same time.

It seemed there was a reason for the shirt after all. I didn't get it though. Was he going for a nighttime jog? A costume party? Having his picture taken for a catalog? I gave him my best "What are you talking about?" face.

"I'm doing laundry," he said. "Would I be wearing this ridiculous shirt if anything else was clean?"

"Why do you even have a shirt you don't like?"

"It was a Christmas present from my parents. I'm sure my mom picked it out. I don't know what she was thinking. Do you like it?"

Even though he already said he didn't like the shirt, I still didn't want to insult him. Or the mother who picked it out. He laughed at my hesitation.

"You can be honest," he said. "I saw the look you gave me when I first walked up."

"What look?"

"You totally did a double take. There was definitely a strong reaction to something. My guess is the shirt. And since you haven't said that you liked it…"

"Maybe I just didn't want to give you a big head by telling you how great you look."

"I look great?"

"I didn't say that."

"Of course you didn't. Because you don't like the shirt."

"I didn't say that either."

"Why won't you just agree that I look ridiculous?"

"Because you don't." He didn't. He looked like someone who was too nice to tell his mom that she only imagined he liked colorful shirts.

The corner of his mouth twitched, trying to hold in a laugh, as he fixed his eyes on mine. "If you don't admit that this shirt is the reason your eyes bugged out when you saw me, then I'm going to start wearing it every time we're together."

My eyes fell to my empty plate in defeat. "I don't *dislike* the shirt," I insisted. "It just… it just doesn't look like you."

Jason sighed. "I'm going to let you get away with that answer. For now."

"What does 'for now' mean?"

"So what are you going to be doing while I'm babysitting washing machines anyway?"

He was going to pretend he hadn't heard my question. I didn't have plans. That was why I had hoped Jason didn't either. "Well," I said, "I have an assignment that I could work on. You know, if I wanted to do an extra good job on it."

Jason stood up to clear his place. "I guess I can assume that you won't be working on it then."

I shrugged and grabbed my stuff, too. We walked out together and waved in the stairwell as I continued up to the 4th floor without him and without the invitation to continue our time together. When I got back to my room, I called Erin to give her some grief over the ill-timed text. She still thought it was funny.

Chapter 21

I had to work on Thursday, and Friday brought with it a different type of work. My accounting class was learning about cash flow statements. We were given a list of numbers that we had to separate into incomes and expenses. Then there was some adding and subtracting, with calculators. It was pretty basic stuff. Until we had to divide ourselves into groups. Distractions never made anything easier.

Rhonda immediately looked at me and asked if I knew what amortization was. The professor had said that we would start working on amortizations in the next class and that it was a way of spreading costs out over time. I told her I only knew that it was a way of spreading costs out over time. She seemed satisfied just to know that she wasn't the only one who didn't understand something before it was taught. Then we worked next to each other without talking while the other two girls talked next to each other without working.

One of those girls had apparently just been dumped by her boyfriend and she spent most of the time listing the reasons she was tired of him anyway. The other girl seemed very knowledgeable about getting tired of guys. Her name was Amy. It looked like Aimee, but it was Amy. Amy rolled her eyes a lot and used the word clueless a lot. I was trying to ignore them and I glanced over at Rhonda to see if she looked annoyed as well. That was a bad idea. It put the song in my head with altered lyrics. Help me, Rhonda. Help, help me, Rhonda. Make these girls shut up.

It was a good thing the professor didn't expect us to finish during class. We were just supposed to get started and then we could finish before class on Monday either with our group or on our own. I wished the group part was optional during class time as well. When it was time to pack up, I breathed a premature sigh of relief. Amy suddenly turned to me and Rhonda and said, "So when are we gonna finish this?"

"Um, he said we didn't have to do it together." I was glad Rhonda spoke up first. I closed my bag and stood up.

Amy stopped me from leaving when she said, "Here's the thing. I kinda bombed the midterm so I need to get a good grade on this."

I just looked at her for a minute. For a talker, she was pretty bad at asking for help. Rhonda said, "Sorry, but I'm going home for the weekend. I'll have to work on it by myself."

"You're going to be gone the whole weekend?" Amy asked.

"It's my dad's birthday."

Amy shrugged at that and Rhonda took it as her cue to leave, along with most of the class. Then Amy rolled her eyes before turning them back to me. "When can you help us?"

Us. Apparently Alison wanted to work together even though she hadn't said anything. She was busy with her phone. "Um, I have to work tomorrow," I said.

"All day?"

"Not until 2 o'clock."

"Well, I don't get out of bed before noon on weekends so that doesn't give us much time. What about Sunday afternoon?"

"I probably have some time on Sunday. Like at 2 or 3 maybe?"

"3 o'clock," Amy said definitively. "We can meet in the lounge upstairs."

"Where's the lounge?" I didn't know there was a lounge in the Business Building. Accounting was the only class I had had there so it wasn't too surprising, at least to me, that I didn't know its ins and outs.

Amy pointed to the stairs outside the classroom while her eyes pointed to the ceiling again. "It's right at the top of those stairs."

I nodded and left the room wondering how my optional group project had become not optional. I also wondered if Rhonda's dad was really having a birthday.

Jason sent me a text on Saturday asking if I had to work. I couldn't respond right away because I was already at work when he sent it. And I was already having a bad day because I had just found out that I was getting a promotion. They made me an assistant manager. I know that sounds like a good thing and I did get to hold a key for the register, which I liked, but it meant that there might come a time when I was supposed to be in charge.

There was always a manager on site, but if he or she was on the phone or otherwise unavailable, then one of my co-workers might need me to be a manager. Just about the only reason anyone would not be able to wait for the real manager would be to deal with an angry customer. Angry people scared me. Angry people who thought I was in charge scared me even more.

Between the bad news at work and the tutoring I hadn't signed up for, my weekend was in need of a bright spot. I was more grateful than usual to be back at church. That morning sitting next to friends in a place where I wasn't supposed to talk felt like more or less the definition of heaven. Jason smelled nice, too. He didn't really seem like a cologne sort of guy so I didn't know if I was just sensing some sort of manly scented cleaning product. But I liked whatever it was. Matt was on my other side with his lovely voice.

Instead of listening to the homily, I got completely lost in the stained-glass window to our right. It depicted a young shepherd carrying a lamb over his shoulders. We had a dog when I was little, a terrier, and my brother used to carry him around like that. I always thought the dog hated it. But he never put up a fight so I was trying to figure out what had made me think that. I couldn't read people. What made me think I could read a dog? I had probably thought the dog hated it only because I would have hated to be up on Andy's shoulders. Just because I was afraid of heights didn't mean that everyone was afraid of heights. I'm not sure I had understood that at the time.

The four of us walked to the dining hall after church. Matt asked me on the way if I had any thoughts on the homily. He was grinning. He had obviously caught me not paying attention.

"Umm… what did you think of it?"

"You don't even know the topic, do you?" he pressed.

I know I looked guilty and Jason said teasingly, "Charlotte, I'm shocked. Were you daydreaming during church?"

"I… how do you know I wasn't praying?"

Matt just looked at me. Jason looked at me. Abby looked at the sidewalk.

"All right," I said. "I was looking at the window. I like the stained-glass. It's pretty."

Matt smiled. "I suppose I can understand being distracted by pretty things." Then he looked at Abby, who kept looking at the sidewalk but turned a bit red. That was sweet. It still made me stare at the sidewalk the rest of the way into the building.

Jason had cereal for lunch. I asked if he had skipped breakfast and he said no, that he just felt like cereal again. Matt and Abby spent most of the lunch debating movie listings. They planned to go out in the afternoon. Jason asked if I wanted to do something with him while they were at the theater. I inwardly cursed that no-longer-optional group project and I think my face showed my revulsion because Jason said, "That bad of an idea, huh?"

"Oh, no. I would love to see you later." I paused for a moment to chastise myself for using the word love instead of like. Maybe it was okay in that context. "I'm just disgusted at the reason I can't."

"What's that?"

"I somehow got roped into doing this accounting project as a group even though the instructor said working together was optional."

"That sucks," he said. "Isn't accounting the class with Help Me Rhonda?"

"Yeah, except that she's not even going to be there to help me."

It took me a few seconds to realize why they all laughed at my frustration. I hadn't said help me to continue the joke on purpose. I figured it out when Matt started singing, "Help me, Rhonda. Help, help me, Rhonda." I couldn't believe the song was still annoying when Matt sang it. I needed to talk so that he would stop.

"Anyway," I said, "she bailed on me, said she had to go home for the weekend, so now I'm stuck trying to explain to this Amy person the difference between money coming in and money going out."

"I hope you do a good job, otherwise her future husband may be in big trouble," Jason said. Matt nodded his agreement.

Only an hour or so ago I had been feeling somewhat mature thinking about an insight I hadn't had as a child. The way my stomach fluttered when Jason said the words future husband made me feel much less mature. I forced myself to stop being ridiculous and focus on reality. "I just hope it doesn't take forever, though I'm sure it will feel like forever regardless."

"What time are you meeting her?"

"Them," I corrected. "Amy was the one who insisted we meet, but I think the other girl will be there, too. 3 o'clock."

"That's still two hours away."

"Yeah, but I have to look over the assignment first. I think the group part will go faster if I already know what I'm doing."

"Okay, but you'll be done in time for dinner," Abby said. "We've decided on a 2:10 show and it'll be done by… then we need to drive back and…" She sort of wiggled her head as though she was literally floating the numbers around in there. "Um, we can all meet right here again at 5:30." She looked around the table for agreement.

Matt nodded. Jason nodded.

I said, "If this project isn't done by then, I probably won't be very good company anyway so I'll just have to eat by myself."

Chapter 22

The lounge in the Business Building was nothing like the lounge on the 4th floor. It wasn't even a room. It was a really wide hallway that ran the length of the building. There were offices lining both sides, all of them closed with windowless doors and the place was almost deserted. There were two rectangular tables at the top of the center staircase as I came up. The rest of the place was furnished only with squashy cubes in different shades of blue. I saw the girl I was meeting who was not Amy. Her name was Alison. She was sitting on one of those blue cubes, thumbs working furiously on the phone in front of her. There only seemed to be two other people in the space that was not a room, two guys with papers spread onto one of the two tables.

I walked over to Alison and waited for her to notice I was standing there. She looked up long enough to acknowledge me and I suggested we grab the other table. She shrugged and followed me to it, not putting the phone down. I sat and pulled the assignment and a notebook out of my bag. Alison sat across from me and didn't look up again. It seemed pointless to start without Amy so we sat there ignoring each other for at least 20 minutes. I was trying to decide if I had waited long enough that Amy wouldn't be able to yell at me for leaving when she came rushing up the stairs.

"Oh, I'm glad you guys are still here. I was totally not paying attention to the clock."

She sat down without opening her bag and asked Alison if she had lined up any new prospects since ditching her deadweight boyfriend. Alison replied that she had a guy on the hook who might have potential. They spent about ten minutes discussing this potential, which sounded entirely physical. Eventually, Amy opened her bag and said we should get the homework over with. But instead of anything accounting related, her phone came out of her bag. She checked and typed out a few messages. I just knew she wasn't reading anything before she sent it. I was about to actually say something when she set the phone on the table and pulled out her assignment. Then she looked at me expectantly.

"Um, well…" I glanced at Alison who had her notebook open next to her phone on the table. Her eyes were still glued to the phone. "The first thing I did was go through the list and mark everything with a plus or a minus for incomes and expenses."

"Okay," Amy said. "Can I see yours?"

I had a feeling that was how this was going to work. One of the many reasons I despised group projects was that sometimes they felt like school sanctioned cheating. It was simply expected that someone would be handing out answers. I refused to let it play out like that, which only made the social aspect of the projects that much more difficult. I said, "Don't you want to know how to do it? It might be on the exam?"

Amy rolled her eyes at Alison, who rolled her eyes right back. Then Amy looked at her list and began to read out the items as she marked them. I had to explain a few things that made keeping my own eyes in place a little tricky. We were nearly halfway through the list when one of the guys from the next table walked over and interrupted.

"Hello, ladies," he said. It was clearly a social hello and not a can I borrow a pencil hello. Amy and Alison returned his greeting with equal disregard for the fact that I didn't want to be there in the first place and it was already after 4 o'clock.

He sat down next to Alison and looked across the table at Amy. "You're in my econ class Tuesday and Thursday, right?"

"Yes," she answered. "I've seen you there."

"I'm Jake."

"I know your name."

He seemed pleased.

"Do you know my name?" she asked.

"Amy Stiplin," he said confidently.

Amy nodded. "Is that all you know about me?"

"No."

"What else do you think you know?"

He glanced at Alison, who had picked up her phone and was ignoring us again. Then he smiled and said, "What would you like me to know?"

"Hmm…" Amy looked up at the ceiling and appeared to be concentrating more than she had been on our accounting homework. "You should know that I'm a business major, otherwise I wouldn't be taking that horrible econ class. And I like lilies."

I grabbed a book out of my bag and stopped listening at that point. The most inane conversation ever now included a gift request from a near stranger. I didn't need to hear any more to know they weren't going to be discussing accounting any time soon. I think I made it through an entire chapter before I realized they were talking about me.

"Her name is Charlotte," I heard Amy say.

I looked up.

"Charlotte," Jake repeated, nodding at me.

"Yes?" I said.

"I was just saying that I thought my friend would like to join us." Jake jerked his head back to the other table in the non-room. There was another guy there and he was looking in our direction.

"Does he know anything about cash flow statements?" I asked, hoping to remind Amy why we were there.

"Actually, he's majoring in accounting." Jake happily and somewhat obliviously waved the other guy over.

The new guy walked over. He was slightly heavy and was wearing a shirt that said, "How many sheep does it take to change a light bulb?" I didn't particularly like shirts that talked either.

"This is Carter," Jake said as the new guy took the seat next to him. "Carter, this is Amy, Charlotte and Alison. Charlotte is interested in accounting."

Carter nodded at me as though I had actually said I was interested in accounting. I was still holding my book and was tempted to go back to reading it. That probably wouldn't help us get the project done so I could leave. I slipped the book into my bag. Perhaps there was a chance I could get Carter to explain things to Amy and then they wouldn't even need me. "The three of us," I moved my head between me and the two other girls, "are taking accounting together and we're working on a cash flow statement."

Carter nodded.

I looked at Amy. "Why don't you show him how far we've gotten?"

Amy pushed her list of numbers towards Carter. He glanced at it, showing about as much interest in accounting as I felt. Then he asked if accounting was my major. I shook my head and said, "English."

Jake and Amy carried the conversation after that. It needed to be carried because it didn't have any legs of its own. Alison was still tapping away at her phone and looking to me as if she was their stenographer. Carter kept looking at me. I kept looking at my watch. It was nearly 5 o'clock when Jake said, "We should do this again sometime."

This? He wanted to do *this* again? He wanted to hijack an already awful group project so that it took longer than forever again. And he was smiling at the suggestion. Talkers would never make sense to me.

He said, "You girls will have to give up some digits so we can arrange it."

Fat chance. I waited to see what Amy would say. She was smiling coyly. "I think you *guys* will need to hand over your numbers," she said. "Makes things more interesting that way."

Jake smiled. "I like interesting."

Amy picked up her phone and prepared to enter his number. I pulled out my phone and pretended to type in Carter's number. Going with the flow seemed the easiest way to get the guys to leave. They stood and went back to their table to collect their belongings. Morbid curiosity made me check out the back of Carter's shirt as he turned around. It said, "I don't know. That's why I'm asking ewe."

Jake waved to us, mostly Amy I think, as they headed down the stairs. I tried to smile politely and not look as though I was hoping to never see either of them again. I rather naively thought we could get back to the task at hand once the distractions had left. Amy looked at Alison, who put down her phone for a whole second. Then Amy said, "Can you believe that?"

"I know!" Alison answered.

"He's so clueless."

"I know."

"He thinks I'm really going to call him."

"I know."

I shook my head when Amy interrupted the I-know-fest to ask if I was going to call Carter. If she had to ask, then Jake wasn't the only clueless person around. I was trying to digest the fact that we had wasted an hour for a guy in whom she wasn't even interested. I reached across the table to grab Amy's copy of the assignment. "So it looks like office supplies is the next thing on our list."

"Yeah, okay. I can't believe how long this project is taking," Amy lamented.

I kept my mouth shut about all the things I couldn't believe, trying to simply be grateful that we were about to move forward again. We got through the list and I pulled out my sample statement because neither Amy nor Alison had thought to bring that and slowly I helped them begin to organize the numbers.

Then Amy's phone rang and she said, "Oh, I have to take this," before jumping up and running to the end of the hall. In the empty space, we could hear every word she said anyway. It sounded about as important as her conversation with Jake. It was 5:40. There was no way I could meet my friends before they finished eating and it occurred to me that they might try to wait for me. I asked Alison if there was a restroom nearby. She said she only knew of the one at the bottom of the stairs. I told her I'd be back in a minute, though I considered bringing all my stuff so I could later pretend I had somehow forgotten to return.

Instead, I brought only my phone. I sent Jason a text from the bathroom. It said: `Sorry I'm missing dinner. I` think I may be a hostage in the Business Building for the rest of my life.

I didn't get a response right away so I went back upstairs to wait for Amy. A bunch of other voices began to cover up her phone conversation as a group of people appeared at the top of the stairs. Five or six people engulfed that formerly abandoned table next to ours, and they were quickly joined by two more guys. It was a loud group and the space felt different with so much life. Oppressing rather than depressing. I wasn't sure it was an improvement.

It was after 6 o'clcok when Amy finally returned to the table. I somewhat impatiently shoved her paper under her nose before she could sideline the project again.

She looked kind of annoyed with me. "All right." She appeared to be looking for where she left off. "So we put rent here," she mumbled. It wasn't a question, but I could see she was writing in the wrong number so I had to say something.

"Um, this is an annual cash flow statement and that's listed as a monthly rent."

"Oh. So we need to, like, multiply by twelve or something?"

I think that was a question. "Yes," I said. "Twelve."

Amy moved her calculator in front of her and Alison did the same. I still didn't know how much Alison was listening. She mostly just copied everything that Amy did.

I sensed that another person was coming up the stairs. I assumed he or she was about to join the big group so I didn't look up. Instead, the person came up behind me and said, “I’ve been looking all over for you. Grab your stuff and let’s go.”

I realized that he was talking to me and that it was Jason. I was so surprised I just said, “What?”

He said, “Come on, we gotta hurry.”

Chapter 23

I scooped everything into my bag and Jason said, "Sorry. It's an emergency," to Amy and Alison as he ushered me down the steps. As soon as we got to the bottom, he turned to me and said, "Don't worry, everything's fine."

I must have had the most mystified expression on my face as I said, "What?" again because Jason started laughing.

"There's no emergency," he said. Then he motioned me into an empty classroom to hide in case Amy and Alison decided to leave as well. I'm not usually quite so slow on the uptake, but three hours of trying to do a group project had sucked me into some sort of stupor. I was starting to see the humor in my escape and in the looks on the other girls' faces as I ran off. But now there was a problem.

"What am I supposed to tell them in class tomorrow when they ask me what happened?"

Jason stopped laughing. "I'm sorry. I didn't think about that."

"Maybe you should have had a better plan."

"Yeah, I didn't really have a plan at all. I just… wait, I think they're coming."

Jason was right. We stood silently against the wall of the classroom listening to the rest of my group leave the building. Their shoes clicked noisily on the stairs, but we could hear what they were saying as they passed. Alison seemed to be trying to convince Amy to call Jake. Her argument was that he might have cuter friends. I wasn't sure if she meant one of them for Amy or for herself. I turned back to Jason once they were out of earshot because he had some explaining to do.

He looked a little embarrassed. "You're not mad at me, are you?"

I wasn't. I said, "I don't know yet," because I wanted to know what had just happened.

"Are you hungry?" he said.

"I am."

"Good. I have food. We can eat and talk."

He gestured to the back row of desks and I sat down while he began to pull things out of his bag. He set a bottle of water on the desk in front of me and another one on the desk next to me. Then he pulled out a paper bag and tipped it towards me. There were three bagels inside. I helped myself to the one on top because it was cinnamon swirl and because it was on top. Jason took out the next bagel and sat down next to me.

"Well…" he started and then he looked at me apologetically. "I don't know what just happened."

"I think you know more than I do."

"Okay, I got your text about being stuck here and missing dinner and everything and well, I thought I'd just drop off some food so at least you wouldn't be starving. And then when I walked in, you looked so miserable I felt like I had to rescue you and, well, I didn't have time to think of a good plan."

"It did work," I admitted.

"So you're not upset with me? I mean, your homework is done and everything?"

"Yeah, I was able to get mine done before the meeting even started. In fact, if you can help me think of something to tell those girls tomorrow, then… you might actually be my hero." I was not exaggerating. Now that I had had a few minutes to get over the surprise, I was very glad that Jason had ended the meeting early. I think he thought I was exaggerating, but he looked okay with that.

He smiled sheepishly, "Did you notice how I brought bread and water? I thought prison food would be funny."

I laughed. I hadn't noticed that. I did notice that he brought enough for my whole group. If he didn't stop being so thoughtful, some girl was going to snatch him up and then I would be in trouble. "This is pretty good for prison food."

"Thanks."

"So what am I going to say tomorrow?"

Jason took a deep breath. "Okay… Let's see… Maybe your roommate got locked out and needed your key because…"

"She could just go to the front desk."

"What?"

"They have extra keys at the front desk."

"They do?"

"Yeah, my freshman year roommate locked herself out like eight times."

"Huh. I didn't know that."

"Have you ever locked yourself out?"

"No. Now that you mention it though I would probably think to check there if I did. Okay, bad idea." Jason worked on his food while he tried to think up a better idea. "I'm thinking it can't be anything medical, right? It's not like you're a nursing student."

"Right. I'm sure you'd come get me so I could slap some Shakespeare on a gaping wound."

Jason laughed. That was good. He always laughed when I was trying to be funny, not like other guys who laughed for no reason. Then he said, "Car trouble, maybe?"

"Um, I'm not a car… fixing… student either. What do they call people in mechanic school?"

"I don't know. But maybe I needed you to give someone a ride?"

"So fast you couldn't explain it? I think that would be a case of needing an ambulance."

"Maybe." Jason looked a bit defeated. I felt bad about shooting down his ideas without coming up with any of my own. But I couldn't come up with any of my own. His face brightened with another thought, "Hey, could you be, like, mysterious about it?"

"What do you mean?"

"Just tell them that you don't want to talk about it?"

"I'm afraid they might think someone died."

"Well… you could be vague. Just say someone you know likes to overreact."

"They would probably think that someone is you."

Jason shrugged. "I don't mind taking one for the team."

I smiled. He didn't mind taking one for the team. We were a team. It was a great plan.

****

Jason and I walked back to the dorm quickly after we finished our prison food. It was officially spring, but it didn't feel like spring. Especially not after dark. He opened the door for me when we got to the building and I returned the favor at the stairwell. The doors to the stairs were always propped open except on the ground floor. I didn't know why that one was different. I walked through after him and he had turned to face me instead of starting up the stairs.

"Charlotte, can I ask you something?"

"Sure."

He looked at the ground. "This really isn't any of my business so you don't have to tell me, but I was just wondering what happened between you and Adam."

"I…" I didn't know what to say. I wanted to know *exactly* what he wanted to know before I revealed too much information.

Jason stopped me anyway. "I'm not trying to pry for details. I just… Okay, so he's actually in one of my classes this semester and it's a big class so he's, you know, way on the other side of the room, but sometimes we talk a bit and I just wanted to make sure I shouldn't be snubbing him on your behalf." Jason looked up briefly and he noticed that I looked either confused or uncomfortable because I was both and he rushed on. "So all I know is that he told me you guys were dating and I mean I could kind of tell something was going on anyway and then, well, I didn't really see you for a while until that day in the lounge when you were really upset and I just wanted to make sure he didn't do something stupid."

"Oh," was all I said for a moment. That day in the lounge that Jason apparently hadn't forgotten about. Now I was even more embarrassed. I was the only one who had done anything stupid that day. "No, don't… that didn't have anything to do with Adam. We barely… I don't know if you could even call it dating. But… honestly, I hoped you had blocked that horrible incident from your mind, but if we're… you brought it up so I should really apologize. I'm sorry I fell apart on you. I…"

Jason shook his head. "Don't be sorry. I just wish I could have helped."

Oh, crap. I was about to get mushy. "You did help. I was… I don't know, I was just going through a hard time in general and I needed a friend. I know we hadn't really been talking, but you still felt like a friend and that helped. I'm glad we've been spending more time together this year. I don't know what I'd do if… I mean, I…" I made myself stop talking. I was about that close, pretend you can see my fingers really close together, to telling Jason that I loved him and he was already looking at me funny. Guys don't like mushy friends. I knew that from Andy. I tried to lighten the situation with a joke. "In fact, Erin better watch out or you'll knock her right out of that best friend position." It was the best joke I could come up with under pressure.

Jason said, "Yeah, that's exactly what I'm trying to do," as he turned to go up the stairs. I knew I screwed up. I expected him to kid back and even though I could hear the sarcasm, I also heard how annoyed he was with me. I was such a girl. Even for a girl, I didn't like talking about feelings. Why couldn't I have just said, "That wasn't Adam's fault," and moved on? That was all Jason wanted. He didn't want to hear me go on about how pathetic I was. He didn't want to hear about how the guy I hadn't seen in nearly three months had been the only friendly shoulder I had to cry on. I followed him up the stairs, kicking myself all the way.

He stopped at the 2nd floor landing and turned back just long enough to say, "See you Tuesday," before he waved and disappeared.

I nodded and continued up to my floor. Abby was watching TV in our room. I went to shower right away so I could think. That was another good thing about evening showers. I heard sometimes the showers got cold in the mornings. I was in there for a long time and didn't run out of hot water. I just replayed the stupid things I had said over and over. Jason had mentioned Tuesday as we parted. That was good and that was bad. It meant we were close enough that a few minutes of awkwardness wasn't going to end the relationship. I should have been able to put it out of my mind. But the comment also ruled out seeing me before then. I tried to remind myself that Tuesday was only two nights away. Logic, however, had no place in the middle of a perfectly good anxiety attack. Even though I was a lot stronger than I had been when Andy's friends made me hide in my room, sometimes I still wished I wasn't so weird.

****

Abby was sitting on her bed eating a bowl of cereal when I woke up the next morning. I got the impression that she had been waiting for me to wake up. My eyes had barely opened before she said, "He's back!"

There didn't seem to be anyone else in the room and she sounded happy so I didn't bother to panic. I may have been too groggy to panic anyway. I decided to sit up and investigate. I investigated by looking at Abby as though I had no clue what she was talking about.

"Your secret admirer is back!" she said. "Go look on the door."

I thought that guy had given up. Or realized that he was mixing me up with someone else… someone who knew who he was. More than wanting to know what the new message was, I didn't like that Abby knew something that I didn't. I got up and opened the door. The whiteboard said, "Charlotte, What do I do?"

I wiped the note off as soon as I read it, even though it didn't bother me the same way the last one had. It just somehow felt private even though I didn't know what it meant. Abby was finishing her cereal standing up and watching me eagerly as I closed the door. "Isn't that romantic?" she asked.

"Is it?" I thought maybe Abby had watched one too many sappy romances. She was very big into the Hallmark Channel.

"Of course! I would love it if Matt left me a note like that."

"You would love it if he wrote 'What do I do?' What does that even mean?"

Abby sighed. "Well, not now. I mean before we were dating I would have loved it. It's obviously someone wanting to know how to get your attention."

Obviously? That did sort of make sense if you combined it with the first two messages. But how did he know I got those? It was entirely plausible that other people around there had the power to erase dry erase markers.

"What are you going to do?" Abby asked.

"I'm going to get dressed and then find something to eat."

Abby rolled her eyes at me. I kind of deserved it because I knew that wasn't what she meant. "All right," I said. "I don't think I can do anything if I don't know who it is and if he doesn't know how to get my attention then…" I threw up my hands to show Abby that it was not my fault that her romantic fantasy wasn't about to play out.

She looked thoughtful for a moment and then her eyes got big. Almost as big as the Cheshire cat smile that covered her face at the same time. "Speaking of Matt," she said. "What if it's Jason?"

I laughed. "It's not Jason."

"It could be."

I shook my head. It was true that I never knew what people were thinking and sometimes I didn't understand the signals. But guys tended to be kind of conspicuous about that sort of thing. I saw the way they looked at me when they hit on me. Jason didn't look at me like that. And I remembered the way Adam's expression had changed when his feelings changed. Jason still looked at me exactly the way he had that first day we watched Family Feud together.

"But what if it is?" Abby persisted.

I did not like where this conversation was headed. I was sure she was about to ask me how I would feel if it turned out that Jason had been the one to write I love you on our door. If she got any hint at how happy that extremely unlikely scenario would make me then she would almost certainly tell Matt who would tell Jason and that would corner him in the same way Adam had cornered me. I decided to lie. I told myself I was doing it for Jason's sake.

"Look, I think I might know who it is."

"Really!?" Abby's eyes got even bigger than before. She couldn't believe I had been holding out on her.

"There's a guy in one of my classes who's kind of tried to talk to me a couple times recently. And, well, I think I'm just going to end up having to hurt his feelings so that's why I didn't want to talk about it. Can you please promise me you won't tell the guys about this?"

"All right. Are you sure you're not interested?"

I nodded.

"Well, I still think the notes are romantic."

“Okay.” She could think that if she wanted to. I actually did need to get dressed and find something to eat because my first class was less than an hour away.

I had accounting that afternoon. Amy and Alison were far less interested in my so-called emergency than they were in the guy who told me about it. Amy said that she was not surprised that I wasn’t interested in Carter when I already had a hottie of my own. I knew Jason was a good-looking guy. I didn’t like the reminder that other girls might think so, too. I let them think he was my boyfriend. I hoped he was okay with me taking a bit of liberty with his taking one for the team. Not that I had any intention of telling him.

Amy said goodbye to me as we left the room after class. I didn’t think she had ever done that before. It was like she thought maybe I wasn’t such a loser after all. She annoyed the heck out of me so I couldn’t figure out why her sudden approval would matter. It did.

Chapter 24

I had been trying to teach Matt how to shuffle the cards the way I did. He thought it looked cool and no, I never shuffled them on his hand to make him think that. I think he had another failed attempt that Tuesday because he and Abby were picking Tichu cards up off the floor when I entered the lounge.

"Hi, guys," I said.

Abby smiled at me and Matt said, "I don't know what I'm doing wrong."

"I might just be a bad teacher."

Then Jason walked in. If I had had any doubts at all about Abby's theory on who was leaving notes for me on our door, those doubts would no longer have fit in the room. Guys who were interested in me asked for my phone number. They stared at me and laughed when nothing was funny. And they sent giant bouquets of flowers that made my dad institute the completely unnecessary no-dating-before-you're-seventeen rule. They did not wear ridiculous shirts to prove a point. Jason was clearly in friend territory when he showed up in that flashy red-collared shirt less than a week after laundry day.

I resolved to say nothing about the shirt no matter what. Matt apparently did not have the same motivation. The first thing he said was, "Dude, what are you wearing? I thought you hated that shirt."

I had never heard Matt call anyone Dude before so I knew his response to the stripes was nearly as strong as mine. I had to bite my lip to keep from laughing. Jason casually said, "I thought I'd give it another chance because Charlotte really likes it."

Matt's jaw dropped as he turned to me. "Dude, seriously?"

Now I was Dude. That shirt was worse than I thought. I swallowed hard to try to push the laugh down. "I didn't exactly say that."

Matt looked a little confused. He turned to Abby for support. "Tell Jason that shirt makes him look like, I don't know, like a colorblind zebra or something."

We all laughed, even Jason, and we weren't laughing at his shirt. At least not entirely.

"A what!?" Abby said.

Matt was still laughing. He held up his hand. "Wait, this is better…"

"No way." Jason cut him off. "You already had your chance to insult my shirt. Your turn, Charlotte. Take your best shot."

I just shook my head and said, "It's fine."

Abby said, "I don't think you're going to do better than 'colorblind zebra' anyway. That makes so much sense."

I didn't intend to try. We sat down and Matt began to deal out the cards. As Jason picked up his hand, he winked at me and said, "For now." I thought I had probably not seen the last of Jason's wardrobe monstrosity. One way in which I was not weird was that I usually liked to be right about things. I still could not say that I was hoping to see the shirt again.

I did not see it on Wednesday, which was pretty quiet except for that moment in accounting when Amy asked me how things were going with Jason and all I said was fine. I didn't know what she wanted to hear and I didn't have anything to tell. I had to work that evening and there were no angry customers.

I did not see the shirt or its owner on Thursday either. The worst thing that happened that day was that I accidentally made eye contact with a professor and she called on me even though both of my hands were clearly on the desk. I hated when that happened. I also got a text from Erin that said: `It is a truth universally acknowledged that I will never beat Devon.`

Erin had been playing second fiddle, or rather cello, to Devon for about a year and a half now. I assumed her text meant that she had lost another challenge. I didn't know how to console her so I just sent back: `I'm sorry. You're still very good.`

I knew it was kind of lame, but she thanked me anyway. I hoped she had someone on site who was better at making her feel better. Surely her non-fictitious boyfriend would step up.

Amy asked me about Jason again on Friday. I don't think she appreciated the consistency of my answer. I didn't appreciate her attempts to glean information that was none of her business so we were even. Erin sent me another text, something about flowers and bad poetry, which made me think the non-fictitious guy was at least trying. I had dinner alone in my room. I never ate by those window tables anymore. I either ate in my room or with friends. Or both, if Abby happened to be in the room at the same time.

When I finished eating, I took my phone over and sat on the edge of my bed, reminding myself forcefully of Alison as I typed out note after note. The big difference being that I was reasonably sure she actually sent out all the messages that she typed. I wanted to see Jason and didn't know how to suggest it. We hadn't been alone since that awkwardness in the stairwell and I still couldn't get it out of my head. Attempts at casual messages gradually morphed into the things I wished I could say. My typing went something like this.

`Sorry I got mushy on you the other day. And sorry this is mushy, too. Want to meet me in the lounge anyway?`

Delete.

`Have you forgiven me for being a moron? I'm not busy tonight.`

Delete.

`Why haven't I heard from you since Tuesday?`

Delete.

`Am I too clingy to want to see you again already?`

Delete.

`Would it be easier if you felt the same way about me?`

Delete.

`I love you and I'm tired of being careful. Now it's your turn.`

Delete.

`Why don't you miss me yet?`

Send.

Wait! Send? That was the wrong button. What did I just send? I looked to see what I'd sent and tried really hard not to panic. `Why don't you miss me yet?` That might be okay. I could play that off as a jokey message. Maybe. Too late. I was panicking. Texts were usually great because there was time to think about what to say. There was no blurting in print and somehow I had managed to blurt anyway. What was Jason going to think? Should I send something else or wait for his response? I didn't know. I couldn't think over all the panicking and over all the telling myself that I was an idiot.

I jumped when the phone buzzed in my hand. For a few seconds, I was afraid to check the message. I exhaled slowly and took a peek. Jason had responded with: `Hang on a second.`

What did that mean? At least he responded. I thought that was probably good. I waited to see if another text was coming. A short time later a second text said: `Okay, NOW I miss you. Meet me in the lounge?`

That was kind of funny. He must have thought I was joking, too. I could relax now. I said: `I'll be there in a minute.`

I picked up a game called *Lost Cities*. It was a two-player game that Andy had given me for Christmas. I played it once with him before coming back to school and once with Abby. She didn't like it. Maybe Jason would like it so much that he'd want to play it all the time and since it only worked with two people and it was my game… don't you see how that would be perfect? Or at least helpful? I was starting to think maybe I needed some help.

I was not surprised that Jason showed up in the lounge right after me wearing that stupid red shirt again. Why was he being so stubborn about that? I was never going to admit I didn't like it. Yes, that was mostly because he was trying so hard to make me. And no, it's not the same kind of stubborn at all. I simply smiled and said, "Hi."

"Hey, Charlotte." He nodded at the table in front of me. "New game?"

"Sort of. I got it for Christmas."

"Have you had a chance to play it yet?"

"Only twice. It's for two players so it's no good for Tuesdays and Abby didn't like it."

"Okay." Jason sat down and I handed him the instructions. "You're not even going to try to teach me?"

"Just read it. It's not very long and I don't want you to blame me when you lose."

"*When* I lose. Let the trash talking begin."

I shrugged. I meant to say if. But he was smiling so he didn't need to know that. I watched him reading the instructions. I liked that I could pretty much stare and his eyes were too busy to notice. I noticed that he had a blue T-shirt under the one I wasn't going to mention. I had a strong suspicion that he had added the top layer after he knew we were meeting. His eyebrows scrunched together in the middle as he was reading the back page.

"Um," he said, "Are we going to need a calculator to keep score?"

"It's not as complicated as it looks. It'll make sense after the first round."

Jason looked back at the scoring example uncertainly.

"Don't worry," I said. "If you get stuck, I can just tell you who wins."

"I don't think I trust you enough to do that."

I tried to look offended. "Are you accusing me of having a history of lying?"

"You told me you didn't dislike this shirt and you said it was fine. I think that establishes a pattern."

"Unless I was being honest both of those times."

"You were not. I know you hate this shirt as much as I do and I don't know why you won't admit it."

"You know, the more you wear it the more I really am starting to get used to it."

"Are you kidding?" Jason eyed me carefully. I don't think he knew whether I was or not.

I shook my head. I was the biggest liar ever. But Jason was the one who started this battle of wills.

He sighed, sounding more than a little disgusted. "All right! You win," he said. Then he pulled the shirt over his head and tossed it inside out onto the chair on his other side. He looked up at me. "You will never see the shirt again. Are you happy now?"

I was happy. After all, I won. And now Jason was looking great again in a nice, plain blue shirt with blue eyes that said I was driving him just a little bit nuts. Life was good. I could toss him a little consolation prize. I said, "Would you like me to throw that out for you?"

He laughed and picked the shirt up again. For a second I thought he was going to throw it at me. I think he was thinking about it. Instead he put it back down and said, "No, I'll keep it in my closet for a while and then donate it somewhere."

I opened up the game board and started shuffling the cards.

Jason said, "Great, now you made me forget how to keep score already." He picked up the rules again.

He did a fine job learning the rules because he beat me the first game. Then I won the second. Each game took no more than 30 or 40 minutes so we were about to start a third as a tie-breaker.

We had been talking about the movie that Matt and Abby had seen the previous weekend and Jason was shuffling slowly. "Matt seemed to really like it," he said. "He's almost convinced me that I should go see it."

"Really? Are you looking for a date?" I didn't know what made me say that. That's not true. I knew. I was hoping he'd reassure me that there wasn't anyone he was hoping to date. But as soon as the words were out of my mouth, I realized that it might sound like I was volunteering. "Not that there's anything wrong with seeing a movie by yourself," I added, very smoothly.

"Well," Jason started to deal the cards, "I was going to ask if you were interested. Unless you'd be bothered that they didn't follow the book enough."

Yeah, I'd be bothered because I was an English major and not because I'd have to spend the whole time reminding myself that it wasn't a date. "I could probably keep my complaints to myself."

"Okay. Are you working Saturday or Sunday?"

"Sunday."

"Okay, we'll go tomorrow."

It was only after we settled on a time that I thought it was sort of strange that he already knew what times it was playing. He must have wanted to see the movie more than he was letting on. And I didn't blame him for not wanting to go alone. That looks like you can't get a date, not that you don't want a date. At least that's what Erin had told me.

I was celebrating my tie-breaking victory, internally for the most part so as not to rub it in, when Matt found us and sat down at the table. He wanted to play and Jason taught him. He made it sound easy. Not the game, the teaching someone how to play the game. He beat Matt soundly the first time and then I beat Matt, too. He demanded rematches from both of us and I lost track of how many times I played and how many times I watched.

We were in the lounge until just after 1 am. Matt was trying to talk either of us into one last game when a group of guys came into the room. They had obviously been drinking. They were talking loudly, one of them sort of fell onto the couch instead of sitting on it and two of them were carrying bags that made me think the "party" was going to continue in the lounge.

We put away the game as fast as we could and I picked up the box while Jason picked up his shirt and the three of us walked out without saying a word. Unfortunately, one of the intruders did say something, something vulgar about me sticking around to be their… well, there isn't a nice way to say it. We were a few steps outside the door when the comment reached us. Matt and Jason immediately turned around as if to go back in and I grabbed each of them by an arm and hissed, "No!"

They stopped and looked at me in disbelief. Jason whispered, "You think we're gonna let him…"

"Yes. Violence is never the answer."

Jason rolled his eyes at the cliché. Matt pulled his arm out of my hand. I grabbed him again. "Wait! There are five of them and two of you. It is not a good idea to say something!"

Jason looked like maybe he was about to come to his senses and Matt said, "Oh, but I know what is. Come on!" He raced down two flights of stairs with me and Jason on his heels. When we got to the 2nd floor he began to explain. "That guy lives on our floor and I know which room is his." The two guys ducked into the bathroom before I could hear the rest of the plan. I had a bad feeling that going into the bathroom was part of the plan. They reappeared moments later with toilet paper, two rolls each.

"Guys, what are you doing?" It felt like a bad plan.

Jason said, "You'll see."

I did see. I saw them get down on their hands and knees and begin unrolling the toilet paper while pushing it under the door to room 207. I felt a panic far worse than when I worried about saying something I'd regret. Matt asked me to be lookout and I gladly and selfishly went down the hall to listen for the stamping of feet on the stairs or the ping of the elevator. They thought they were defending my honor or something so I felt bad that I didn't want to be standing near them if they got caught.

It was probably not more than ten minutes that I stood in that quiet hallway. Each of those minutes made my heart go faster. When they finished and motioned me toward them, I ran down the hall and already felt like I had run down a thousand halls. I was not cut out for mischief-making.

The stairs in the building were actually north and south and not front and back, but I always thought of the one by the lounge as the front because that was the one I always used. That night we went up the back stairs, still running. I was in a hurry to get behind the locked door of my room and I wanted Matt and Jason safely behind theirs as well. I said good night and Matt asked if he could borrow the game I forgot I was holding because he was too wired to sleep anyway. I handed it over and said good night again.

Chapter 25

There were a lot of reasons that I felt awful in the morning. I had not been able to bring myself to shower in the middle of the night. Or even go to the bathroom to brush my teeth. So I got into bed feeling gross and unable to sleep. I think it was close to 5 o'clock before I managed to drift off. That meant that I slept much later than usual, waking up at a time you could only barely call morning and with a sharp headache. I squinted myself over to my shower bucket. Abby was sitting at her desk reading a book. She sort of nodded a good morning and otherwise left me alone.

The hot water helped a bit. Just as I was starting to relax into it though, water turned on next door and a voice said, "Hey, who's over there?"

I didn't do small talk while I was naked so I didn't answer. The few other times that had happened, playing mute had gotten the hint across.

"Hey, you, in the corner stall… I'm talking to you."

It didn't look like I was going to be so lucky this time. I continued to ignore her, but it was not helping me relax which I needed to do to help the headache loosen its grip on my skull.

And then I saw a hand grab the top of the divider on the side where the benches are. I realized what was going on and turned my back just as a head popped up and said, "Oh, it's you."

Yeah, *it's me.* What she had just done would be considered criminal if she were a guy and yet she clearly thought I was the weird one for not wanting to carry on a conversation about nothing that we'd have to yell to have over the water and while I was, that's right, still naked. But at least now that she knew it was me she didn't try to talk anymore.

I passed Abby in the hall on my way back to the room. She told me that she was going to meet Matt for lunch if I wanted to join them. I told her not to wait on me because I needed to try to dry my hair. It took forever and I didn't even get it all the way dry, just dry enough that I no longer looked like a drowned rat. I had more trouble deciding what to wear than usual. I was going out with Jason that afternoon and it was not a date. I wanted to find something that said I knew it wasn't a date, and still said that it would be okay if he wanted to think it was. Sadly, my clothes didn't talk either. None of them said anything remotely like that. I settled on a dress that was light pink. I think someone whistled at me last time I wore it and Jason had seen it before so maybe he wouldn't think I was trying too hard.

I was dressed and had an hour left before I had to meet Jason and I was starving. I knew exactly what to do with that hour.

I scrounged up some brunch foods, including slightly dry scrambled eggs, and took a tray back to my room. Matt and Abby weren't at any of our usual tables so I figured they had left.

I turned the TV on while I ate and found an episode of Family Feud. I had always just liked that show sort of okay until the day I watched it with Jason. I thought about that first day and how I had wanted him to talk to me. I was nearly positive that was the only time I had sat down next to a stranger not hoping to be completely ignored. My thoughts were interrupted by a knock at the door. No one ever knocked on my door. Except people who then ran away. I jumped up to the peephole. It was Jason. Why was he picking me up? I was supposed to meet him by the front doors. That was how it worked when something was not a date. I thought maybe I should explain that to him except that I knew what people said when someone protested too much. Then I thought maybe I should open the door. He was likely beginning to wonder what was taking so long when even someone with Abby's short legs could cross the entire room in about four steps.

"Hi," I said.

"Hi. I left my room a bit early so I thought I'd come up and see if you were ready instead of standing around in the lobby. Are you busy?"

"No, um…" I looked at my watch. We wouldn't need to leave for at least 15 minutes. I knew that because I had been watching the clock, but Jason didn't need to know that I had been watching the clock. "Do you want to come in for a bit?" I bit my lip uncertainly. I wasn't expecting company and I didn't know whether or not I wanted him to say yes. Also, in all the time I'd known Jason, he had never been *in* my room, only at the door.

"Sure," he said, "I've never been in your room."

I stepped back and he quickly closed the door behind himself. I thought he seemed a bit eager. Turned out that was because he had something he wanted to tell me. "Okay, so the reason I left my room early is because the guys down the hall had their door open and I could hear them arguing about the mess and I suddenly got this fear that I was going to burst out laughing and then they'd know that I knew something."

"Oh, no! I forgot about the roommate. That wasn't fair to…"

"Don't feel sorry for the roommate. He was in the lounge last night, too, and was guilty by association. Anyway, they were arguing about whose fault it was and which one of them should clean it up and well, they both just seemed so sure that the other one had done it. It's not as funny now that I'm not listening to it."

Jason took a breath and I noticed his eyes moving around the room a bit. I thought it was best if I kept him talking instead of looking. And I was a little confused anyway. I said, "But if they were both in the lounge, how did they think one of them was responsible?"

"Sounded like neither of them could remember last night very well. That's part of what made the argument funny. They weren't making a lot of sense."

"I think they must have spent more time arguing than it would have taken to clean it up. I mean, I know you guys used a few rolls, but it was just toilet paper. You pick it up and stick it in a garbage can."

"Um," Jason winced and looked at the floor. He didn't say anything else. He looked extremely guilty about something.

I took a step closer to try to block his view of the carpet and said, "What did you do?"

He looked over the top of my head instead. "I know you didn't want us to do anything, but he totally deserved it."

I put my hand on his chest as though I was anywhere near strong enough to pin him to the door before I repeated myself. "What did you do?"

"Matt and I, after we dropped you off, we decided that dry toilet paper would be too easy to clean up."

"Dry?"

"Yeah, so we, um," Jason was looking everywhere but at me. My plan to distract him from the fact that I hadn't made my bed and that several rejected clothing choices were still piled on top of it was not working very well. I really wanted to know what they had done so I let his eyes wander while I waited. "Okay, we squirted shampoo under the door. And maybe some toothpaste, too."

"Eww."

"And I think they kind of stumbled around in it last night."

"Eww, again. You guys are terrible."

"I know." Jason hung his head and I detected a bit of actual remorse so I took a step backwards. Out of the mush zone. Just in case. He said, "Matt wanted to play *Lost Cities* one more time and it took longer than all the other games we played. We kept having to remind each other to take a turn. I thought that was because it was the middle of the night, but then I couldn't sleep anyway."

"I'd say it was your guilty conscience except that I had trouble sleeping and *I* didn't do anything."

"You're not too tired to see a movie?"

I shook my head. Then I shook off the strange feeling that the question he was asking was more complicated than the one I was answering. I grabbed my sweater and my purse and Jason opened the door for me. He asked if I had my key before he locked it behind us. I believed he had never locked himself out.

Jason paid for my ticket, which he said was because the movie was his idea. That made sense. That didn't make it a date any more than me buying a ticket for Abby would have been a date. I still wondered why he felt the need to state the reason. Was I not being as careful as I thought I was? Was he worried about me getting the wrong idea?

I let Jason choose our seats because I wanted to sit in an aisle seat and it would have been rude to plop myself on the end of a row and then make Jason climb over me. But I didn't actually say I wanted an aisle seat so he moved closer to the middle of the row and then I had to follow him. Fortunately, the theater wasn't very crowded. No one came to sit on my other side.

I was still kind of uncomfortable because the armrest between us was up and the one on my other side was down. I didn't enjoy being lopsided and I would have preferred that small barrier to help keep Jason from sensing that I was getting all sorts of wrong ideas.

I was still thinking about the armrests when the movie started. I flipped up the one on my left so at least I wouldn't be lopsided. A few seconds later, Jason pushed up the one on his right. He gave me an understanding nod and our eyes met for a second before he turned back to the screen. If there had been any part of my heart that didn't already belong to him, it would have jumped over the nonexistent barrier and settled in his hand.

I tried to watch the movie, but decided I'd rather make my own. I closed my eyes and pictured walking out of the theater with Jason. Some faceless guy approached us and Jason put his arm around me to show him he didn't have a chance. The guy turned away and Jason realized he liked his arm where it was. By the time we made it to my car, he appreciated that I could be more than a friend to him. He wouldn't let us drive off until he kissed me.

It was a beautiful fantasy. And it made me sad.

I don't think the lights were coming back on yet. I think it was just the other people moving about that woke me up. Credits were rolling on the big screen. I had been worried that watching a movie with Jason would feel like a date. I had never considered that it might also feel like a nap. I was a little embarrassed to have been sleeping in public. I looked over at Jason and he had a slightly dazed expression on his face. I said, "Were you sleeping?"

He looked confused. "I think only for a few minutes."

The way he stretched when he stood up made me think it might have been longer. We talked about it on our way out of the theater, trying to decide based on the last scenes we remembered which of us had fallen asleep first. It might have been me. But Jason said he hadn't noticed me sleeping and that was what I really wanted to know.

The walk to the car was uneventful. Nothing happened that made Jason want to put his arm around me. Not that that surprised me. As we were putting on our seatbelts he said, "I wonder what Matt will think."

"What do you mean?"

"I picked the movie based mostly on his recommendation. I wonder what he'll think when I tell him we missed half of it."

"Um..." My first thought was that he would think we missed half of it because we were doing something other than sleeping. But I didn't say that. I just daydreamed for a few seconds and then refocused my attention to the car I was starting so that I could drive safely.

Jason's behavior on the way back was peculiar. It was as though he was being quiet on purpose instead of just being naturally quiet. I wasn't sure how I knew the difference and I was even less sure how I knew that it was my fault. It was my fault though. I was spending too much time on the dream in my head and not enough on the real friendship I had worked so hard to attain.

The afternoon was reasonably warm. I asked Jason if he would be interested in trying to improve my Frisbee skills. He looked more surprised at my suggestion than I was. I knew Frisbee was something that Jason enjoyed. A good friend would be better at suggesting things the other person enjoyed. He went up to his room to get a Frisbee and came back with two of them and his brother.

Matt called Abby from the lawn and eventually talked her into joining us. She was a bit more coordinated than I was – probably from all the dancing – but still not terribly experienced. It worked out well that she and I could practice together while the guys chased much more capable throws from each other.

I did pair up with Jason eventually and he complimented my improvement. I think he was getting a bit tired at that point so he found my improved throws a nice break from Matt's powerful ones. I had fun, too. The best part was that there was absolutely nothing romantic about Frisbee. For the first time that day I thought about how glad I was to have Jason's friendship without thinking there was anything only about it.

****

I think Tichu had become Jason's favorite game as well because on Tuesday Abby tried to suggest we do something else for a change. I thought that was a good idea, but both of the guys were very insistent on Tichu. It ended up being the longest game we had ever played. We were at least two hours into it when Abby said she needed a bathroom break. It was Matt's turn to deal and I think he had finally managed to bridge the cards. He was sitting there practicing and even though a few cards popped out, they all stayed on the table.

Jason ran his hands through his hair and said, "I need a haircut."

I said, "Don't look at me."

He laughed. "I wasn't asking. I was just making an observation."

That's when I decided to make the same observation. My mom always said, "You see with your eyes," when I was little to remind me not to touch things that did not belong to me. I guess that was one time I didn't listen to her. I couldn't help myself. I had wanted an excuse to touch his hair since that day I decided he was sunshine yellow. I moved my chair just a little so I could run my fingers along his scalp.

Jason closed his eyes as though it was relaxing to have someone messing up his hair. "It does seem longer than usual," I said. I didn't say that it was just as soft and inviting as I had pictured. I didn't say it, but I thought it. Then I thought that I should hurry up and relocate my hand before Jason noticed all the sparks flying from my fingertips. But I didn't want to. I didn't know when I might get another chance. I even let the tip of my finger trace the outline of his ear.

And then I remembered where I was and that Jason might not be the only one to notice. I sat back quickly and glanced at Matt. He was resolutely keeping his eyes on the cards he had begun to deal. But he had a knowing look on his face. I chanced a glimpse at Jason. He looked stunned. I put my fingers over my face in case there was any trace left of those feelings I had been hiding forever. Months of being careful had been ruined in about three seconds. Why couldn't I keep my hands to myself?

I hoped neither of the guys were freaking out. We were all still friends. I wasn't going to ruin anything. If they needed proof I could confess how long I had been not ruining anything. I hoped that wouldn't be necessary. I didn't want Jason to feel awkward. I hoped that if I acted like nothing happened, they might think they imagined what they thought they saw.

Abby returned to the room and I tried to cover my embarrassment and get us back to the game by asking to see the score. Jason was keeping score and he slid the paper over to me. The columns were definitely longer than usual, but both teams were getting close. The game was going to end soon one way or another. I was pushing the paper back when I recognized my name.

The rest of us kept score with initials, but Jason liked to write out our names. I don't know why. I did know that I had seen my name written like that before. I was thinking about freaking out because I knew exactly where I had seen my name written like that. It was the first time I ever thought of freaking out as a good thing. I finally understood that Jason was just as bad at communicating with people as I was. I didn't know because he didn't tell me.

I couldn't concentrate on the game after that. I think it showed. Abby was giving me a hard time about something I played.

I said, "You know, I'm starting to think you were right to call me an idiot."

"That's not what I said."

I wasn't talking to Abby, but I said, "It was implied."

She laughed. We won after the next hand so she told me she took back the implication. We didn't have much time to celebrate because Matt packed up the cards and quickly told Abby he wanted to take a walk. I wondered what he was going to tell her once they left the room.

I also wondered if Jason would say something about what he must have noticed. He didn't know that I had finally put two and two together with the score sheet. I thought again how he had been right to imply that I was an idiot. But neither one of us said anything. We just sat at that round table not saying anything. I thought maybe one of us should say something.

I stood up and said, "I guess the game's over." Always a master of conversation, I was.

Jason nodded and he stood up, too. He stayed quiet.

I knew I wasn't imagining that he wanted to kiss me. I didn't know how to tell him that I knew, how to tell him that no one had to be careful anymore. I tipped my head up so my eyes met his. I hoped this was one of those times he could tell what I was thinking. But his eyes were too much for me. I looked at his hands instead. They were on the back of a chair. I tried looking up again and my eyes only made it to his mouth. I looked back down. I watched his feet step closer to me. I watched his hand reach for mine. It stopped only for a second and then brushed all the way up my arm and into my hair. I understood why his eyes closed when I touched his scalp. It sent shivers down my back. And up again.

Finally, Jason said something. "Please tell me I didn't imagine that."

Imagine what? The look on my face when I put my hand in his hair? The goose bumps on my arms at his touch? The fact that my eyes were dancing back and forth between his mouth and lots of inanimate objects around the room? Could I be any more obvious? Well, I could if I said something. I was afraid of ruining the moment, but Jason seemed to be waiting, giving me time to say something. I opened my mouth before I had completely decided what to say and that isn't usually good. "Um, I forgot to be careful."

"What do you mean?" Jason didn't lean in for the kiss I wanted. He didn't back away either, but he looked worried.

"I didn't want to spoil things. I didn't know… I mean, I just saw the score sheet."

"Charlotte, you're not making any sense."

"I didn't know it was you."

"You didn't…" The puzzled expression only lasted a moment before Jason flashed a nervous smile. His hand was still in my hair. I could feel the fingers at the back of my neck tighten a little as he said, "I thought you were pretending not to know so you wouldn't have to reject me."

That sounded like something I'd do. I shook my head as I repeated myself. "I didn't know."

Jason finally started to lean in and I put my hand on his chest to make him wait. I asked him if he'd make me a promise first.

He said okay but he looked like he didn't want to wait.

I was going to make him promise that it wouldn't change anything, that we'd still be friends. But I knew I didn't have to. I knew it would change things and that we'd still be friends anyway. So instead I said, "Next Tuesday, when I suggest a different game, you're going to back me up, right?"

The mouth I was still watching formed a familiar smile. Then he whispered, "No way," right before he kissed me anyway. What followed were a few of the best moments of not talking ever. A lot of wonderful things were said in those few moments. And then we really talked.

Abby was waiting for me when I made it back to my room that night. She didn't say what Matt told her, but she looked like she was expecting news. She said, "So you and Jason are…" Her eyebrows went up to finish the question.

I nodded and I think I turned a bit red.

"I was right about the notes?"

I nodded again and Abby was satisfied. She let me leave to shower. She was still grinning stupidly when I got back. I think I was, too.

We played *Ticket to Ride* on Tuesday. Matt could tell he was outnumbered before Jason took sides. The housing forms came in the mail on Friday. I checked the box. Abby checked the box, too. Then I took some homework into the lounge. Everyone does homework on a Friday evening, right? I didn't look like I wanted an excuse to be in the lounge at all.

My phone buzzed as I sat down. Erin said: `Now I'll always think of Ben whenever I have lemonade. I'm not telling you why.`

I laughed and typed out: `Everything makes you think of Ben. I know exactly why.`

I was still trying to organize some thoughts for an essay when three girls walked in. They had been laughing, but stopped when they saw me and walked back out. I recognized one of them as someone whose room was near mine and who was always trying to start a conversation with anyone and everyone who happened to be in the hallway. I knew she thought I was weird. They had only just left the room when Jason came in. He was carrying some books and he looked good in black. He waved and sat down next to me at that round table. I loved how we didn't have to talk to know we'd both end up in the 4th floor lounge.

More Romantic Comedies by Amanda Hamm

Weathering Evan (2012)

Tightening the Knot (2009)

Dear Jane Letters (2007)

Her Other Titles

Double Take: My First Year as a Mother of Twins (2010)

Zero Station: A Science Fiction Novella (2007)

www.ingramcontent.com/pod-product-compliance
Lightning Source LLC
LaVergne TN
LVHW041925090826
845145LV00015B/692
* 9 7 8 0 9 8 5 0 6 5 9 3 5 *